KT-450-397

30131 05761764 6
LONDON BOROUGH OF BARNET

Published by Knights Of
Knights Of Ltd, Registered Offices: 119 Marylebone Road, London,
NW1 5PU www.knightsof.media

First published 2021
001

Set in Mrs Eaves XL Serif Nar OT Regular / 12 pt
Typeset by Marssaié Jordan
Design by Marssaié Jordan
Printed and bound in the UK

A CIP catalogue record for this book will be available from the British Library

ISBN: 9781913311162

2 4 6 8 10 9 7 5 3 1

HAPPY HERE

INTRODUCTION

What makes you happy? Seriously happy, I mean. So happy that you smile so hard your big grin stings a bit as it stretches across your face, making your eyes squint and shine? *That* happy. So happy, someone annoying might say, *if the wind changes your face will stick like that?*

It won't by the way. Don't listen to them.

But do think about your happiness for a moment. While you wonder, here's what currently brings me joy.

These days, for me, eating something really spicy, so fiery it burns all the way down, makes me incredibly happy. Chilli sweats are a whole vibe. Sleeping too – phew, I love a good snooze under a blanket on the sofa. But my favourite thing, the one that really beats everything else by miles, is getting to write stories for young people, and being able to share them with the world.

That is incredibly important to me. This is why.

Many (many, many) years ago, in the eighties and nineties, when I was a kid, one of my favourite things was cycling around town with my friends and my girl Tropicana – my neon green and pink mountain bike. My first love. My favourite 'trick' was attempting to ride without holding her handlebars. Basic, I know, but I was so scared trying it. I still have the scar on my arm from the one time I actually did.

Another favourite thing: I was a bridesmaid three times. Three. Apparently, this means I'll never get married myself, but that's OK. These weddings were huge, super-fancy affairs full of brilliantly dressed family from across England, the Caribbean and America. We would congregate, celebrate, gossip and giggle. And eat. Dining and dancing to soca bops, especially with my Granddad at the party bit, was brilliant. He was a good dancer.

These were great times, but my most favourite thing, the one I could do every day, at any time – that really beat everything else – was watching, playing and reading stories.

I loved stories, but I wasn't sure stories loved me back.

I devoured everything I could. Our family was surrounded by stories. I was told tall tales of tabby cats and buried treasure. We shared short stories about snow showers and saving the world. I even read a medical encyclopaedia, more than once – I'm basically a doctor now. I loved all of my books – nothing beats being transported to new and unusual worlds, meeting new people and learning about their lives.

The trouble was, in most of the books we read, I struggled to find *us*.

In the many stories, nothing felt like our lives.

There were rarely any characters that looked or spoke like me, my friends or my family.

We were missing. Black people weren't *really* there. When we were, we were mostly being naughty, rude, making trouble, being in trouble. Suffering, generally. Dying first, or doing the deaths, then doing the time. Don't get me wrong, some of these were great stories – truly excellent – but where were the stories about how funny and fascinating 'normal' life could be? Where were the little Black British girls, on bikes? Where was the love, where was the joy? Where were the Black heroes? I tried to find them, but I mostly failed.

Instead, I found that some of the best stories I was told, were the ones we told ourselves.

The funniest (funny strange, not funny ha-ha) thing about this was, I didn't even realise this was a problem. This was just *how it was*. This was normal.

But *how it was* was wrong, and it should never have been normal. All children, no matter where and who they are, deserve to see themselves being bold and brave in stories – not just bad or broken. At best, that's boring. At worst, it's racist. Seeing ourselves in stories is so important. Do you know why? If you can see yourself, it helps you believe in yourself and your abilities. If you believe in yourself, you can achieve *anything* you want to.

I want that for you, because I know you can do it.

So, that's why I love writing stories. I love telling stories about us, for us, and for everyone else, so they can see and understand that there is way more to being Black than just the colour of our skin and the struggles that come with it. I know the writers and illustrators in *Happy Here* agree with me on this. It's why you're holding this book right now. *Happy Here* is a celebration, and all of you readers out there? Well, you're all invited to this party. We threw it for you, after all. You're going to have such a good time, I promise.

In these pages, you'll find ten incredible stories, with ten stunning illustrations by Black creators that burst with joy, show happiness at home, and are about the love between friends and family. The characters in these stories and illustrations take up space, just by being themselves, by being whoever they want to be and it's the best. Ginormous thanks and kisses to all the writers and illustrators in this book – not only for their incredible work and talent, but also for their energy, dedication and being such inspirational role models. I'm so glad their work is opening up our world. It's both a pleasure and privilege to see their thoughts and ideas.

Happy Here is making change. Change is happening, but we do have a long way to go yet. Did you know that between 2017-2019 only 7% of all children's books published in the UK had Black or Brown characters? That's low and it's sad. Thankfully, organisations like Knights Of, the incredible publishers of this book, and BookTrust and CLPE (the Centre for Literacy in Primary Education) are not only watching this; they are working hard to make sure we have more Black creators, characters and readers. I am so very thankful to them for making *Happy Here* happen.

Finally, massive thank you to all of you, out there, reading *Happy Here* right now. We see you, and we believe in you. I do have a favour to ask; I would love it if *you* started writing your own incredible stories, I need tales to read when I'm even older than I am now. In the meantime, my greatest wish, for all of you, is that you enjoy this book and you're *Happy Here,* happy there, happy wherever you are.

Sharna Jackson

March 2021

A HOUSE LIKE NO OTHER

ALEXANDRA SHEPPARD
ILLUSTRATED BY DORCAS MAGBADELO

Izzy Ferguson held on tight to her dad's hand. She was the only girl in Year Six who still did that. But as the tube whistled through the dark and pulled to a screeching halt at the end of the tunnel, the other passengers rushed to the narrow doors at the same time. If Izzy didn't hold his hand, they'd get separated and she'd be lost forever, rattling around the station with nothing but rats for company.

Probably.

Pops looked down at her and smiled. "Don't worry, Izzy. Just a short walk and we're there."

Then you get to go back home, she thought. Traitor.

They crept up the escalator and made their way out of the tube station. Everything bleeped and swished. All the people looked straight ahead or down at their phones. No one stared at Pops.

In the town they lived in, Pops got a lot of stares because of his dark brown skin and waist-length locs. Izzy and her big bro Dev sometimes got the stares too when they were out with Mum. She's white and they're brown and for some reason certain people can't get their head around that. They stare at them like they are a math's equation they're struggling to solve.

Izzy zipped up her winter coat. After the dozy warmth of the tube, the late October chill hit even harder.

The High Street was heaving with people, even on a Wednesday afternoon. Large shops, with shiny window displays, jostled beside market stalls selling incense sticks, shiny jewellery and the type of fruit Izzy only ever saw in the exotic section of the supermarket. She spotted a crate of wrinkled orange mangoes (her favourite!) and the fragrance was intoxicating. It mingled with the traffic fumes and the smell of BBQ lingering in the air.

All the different people, sounds and smells left Izzy feeling too overwhelmed to be anxious about the two days that lay ahead.

"I'm so jealous of you, Iz!" Pops said, steering them through the crowd with ease. Izzy held on tight to his hand. "I'd love to spend a few days in Brixton with Aunty V. She's the coolest."

There it was. Pops' reminder about where they were headed brought Izzy firmly back to earth.

For the first time in her life (all ten years and seven months of it), Izzy was spending two nights without her parents or big brother Dev. She wasn't pleased about it.

Since Dev moved out last month, Izzy's life had taken a spectacular turn for the worse. It seemed like whatever remained of Izzy's confidence had disappeared when he'd packed up for university.

Dev looked after her every half-term and she got his undivided attention. But with Dev at uni, there was no one to look after Izzy while Mum and Pops were at work. The week-long holiday became yet another thing that filled Izzy with dread.

She wished she could feel as proud of Dev as Mum and Dad did. They both shed a tear when they dropped him off at his new home, even if Dad tried to pretend he had dust in his eye. But it only reminded Izzy what a coward she was.

Dev moved like it was as simple as changing socks.

But Izzy was starting secondary school next year and the thought made her tummy curdle like orange juice mixed with milk. Just the thought of this Saturday's ballet show gave her sleepless nights. Why couldn't she be as brave as her big brother?

They passed a bakery window stacked with the kind of bread and cakes Izzy only ever ate at Gran's house.

"Look, Iz," her dad pointed. "Hardo bread! Isn't that your favourite?"

Izzy grunted in response. Hardo bread was her favourite and it was impossible to find in their local shops at home. But she wasn't about to give Pops the satisfaction of making her smile. Not when he was abandoning her.

Izzy had tried everything to get out of staying with Great Aunty V. She was practically a stranger. The rest of Izzy's Jamaican family gathered at Gran's house for Christmas, Easter and the Summer BBQ. But Great Aunty V never visited. Izzy only heard about her in dribs and drabs over the years.

"Gran said that Great Aunty V is a 'character'," Izzy said. "What does that mean?"

Pops laughed. "It means that she's a very interesting person."

"Is it true that she had a bright yellow car? And that she was a singer?"

"Yeah! She had a Mini Cooper called Martin. And she made a heap of cash doing a pet food jingle back in the 80s. Now she's a Drama teacher, I think."

"Drama? Ugh." That was Izzy's least favourite subject. After what happened at the last ballet show, she never wanted to set foot on a stage again. But Mum insisted she finished the term.

"You begged for ballet classes, Izzy," she had said when Izzy tried to get out of it. "They're paid for and I'm not letting that go to waste."

Izzy couldn't argue with that. She did beg for ballet classes. It was all Lottie's idea, and now after The Incident, her ex-best-friend won't even talk to her in class.

They turned onto a quiet street and left the traffic behind them. Soon, the only sound was the rumble of Izzy's suitcase wheels against the pavement.

"Are you sure I can't stay at home alone, Pops? I wouldn't even think about using the stove or opening the door to strangers or—"

He chuckled. "That's out of the question, kiddo."

"But I can take care of myself!" Izzy said. She realised she was still holding his hand and dropped it quickly.

"Getting out of your comfort zone will do you good," Pops said.

"Mum said the same thing," Izzy muttered.

Pops paused for a second and sighed. "Look, Iz. If you really don't want to stay away from home for two measly nights, your mum and I can work something out. Maybe we can both rearrange our shifts. I'm not sure if it'll work, but..."

If they went back home, Izzy would get to sleep in her own bed with her polka dot duvet. There would be no unknowns. But she could just picture the look on Mum's face when they walked back through the door.

Dev told you to be brave, she thought.

"Iz?" Pops said. "We can make the next train back home if we hurry."

Aren't you sick and tired of always being afraid?

Izzy took a deep breath. "No. I'm going to stay with Great Aunty V."

*

"If memory serves me correctly, Aunty V's place is just... here!"

Izzy looked up at a terraced house much like every other on the quiet street, apart from one thing. Every inch of it was bright yellow. From the roof tiles to the bricks to the garden gate.

And not a subtle yellow, either. It was the sort of colour Izzy imagined astronauts could see from space. Yellow curtains adorned the windows and a yellow brick path led up to the front door. Even yellow rose bushes bloomed in the front garden, their bright petals even louder against the watery grey sky.

Pops smiled. "It's exactly how I remember it."

They walked up the garden path and Pops reached for the door knocker. The front door swung open before he touched it.

"Hello? Aunty V?" Pops yelled. "Maybe she forgot to lock the door behind her."

Izzy folded her arms. "And you want to leave me alone with this woman?"

Pops ignored her. Izzy followed him into the darkened hallway and up a narrow staircase. He pushed open another door (also unlocked) and they walked into a large open plan living room bathed in sunlight. It flooded in through the windows, washing the wooden floorboards with its rays. The sunlight combined with the yellow furniture and yellow walls had a dazzling effect. It was like being inside a buttercup.

It took Izzy's eyes a few seconds to adjust. "But it's cloudy outside," she whispered in awe.

"Cloudy is a state of mind, my dear," boomed a voice.

Izzy spun around to see where it came from. At the other end of the large room a very short, very round older woman stood on a stool at the stove. She stirred a pot that was nearly the same size as her. Like the house, she was dressed top to toe in yellow. She wore a yellow blouse, yellow jeans and a yellow shawl was wrapped jauntily over her shoulders.

"Aunty V!" Pops exclaimed, rushing over to greet her.

A tubby black cat purred in the shard of sunlight pouring through the window.

"Don't be rude, Winston! We have company," Great Aunty V said to the cat. She stepped down from the stool and walked over to Izzy.

"Oh my, Isabelle. You have shot up," she said, looking her up and down. Izzy was a good head-and-shoulders taller than Great Aunty V. "The first time we met, you stained my second-favourite shawl with baby vomit. This is already a vast improvement."

"Call me Izzy, Great Aunty V," she said.

"I beg your pardon? My dear, you will have to be bold and use your voice. I'm a trifle deaf," Great Aunty V said.

But she heard me mutter from across the room, Izzy thought.

"I said, call me Izzy!" She bellowed.

"That's more like it! When you're in this house, speak loud and proud."

"We really appreciate you looking after Iz at such short notice," Pops said.

Great Aunty V smiled and for a second she looked just like Gran. "It is long overdue. Will you stay for dinner, Errol? I've made your favourite."

"I'd love to but I need to catch the next train home. Early start tomorrow," he said. "Oh, and by the way, Aunty V. The front door was unlocked."

"Don't be foolish, Errol. It wasn't unlocked. The house knew it was you."

Izzy and Pops exchanged a glance. "Well, as long as you're sure."

They said their goodbyes, and then Pops was gone. Izzy was well and truly alone for two whole days.

"You must be hungry after that long train journey. Go on, sit! I made your favourite."

Izzy smiled weakly and pulled up a chair at the yellow dining table.

"There you go, sweetness," Great Aunty V said. "Your favourite!"

She presented Izzy with a deep bowl of grey-looking mush. It was the texture of lumpy porridge and the colour of concrete.

Izzy smiled weakly. “Looks delish,” she muttered.

“Thank you, darlin’. I spent all day cooking so mind you don’t waste a drop.”

Izzy scooped up a spoonful of grey mush and swallowed it quickly. Her eyes widened with shock.

“It’s mango-flavoured!” Izzy exclaimed. And not just any old mango, but the ripest and juiciest mango she’d ever tasted. The porridge tasted more like mango than mango itself.

Great Aunty V looked puzzled. “What did you expect, child? I told you I made your favourite.”

Izzy polished off her bowl of mush in record time. She even asked for seconds and thirds.

Once she’d eaten her fill, Izzy pulled out her phone. No signal. “Great Aunty V, what’s your Wi-Fi password? I promised Dev I’d let him know when I arrived.”

Great Aunty V waved her hand. “I don’t bother with any of that nonsense, sweetness. This is a technology-free zone.”

Izzy looked around. There was no television or phone or laptop in sight. “B-but how will I do my homework?”

She cackled. “Child, you and I both know you don’t give a single fig about homework.”

"But how do you do anything without the–"

"Enough, Isabelle," Great Aunty V said sternly.

Izzy gulped. "So what do you do for fun?"

"I read, I sew, I play with the cat. Winston can be the most fabulous company when he isn't in one of his sour moods, like today."

"Mi-aow!" came the sharp rebuttal from Winston. He was curled up on the mustard yellow sofa.

"I'm sorry about him," she whispered. "He's not used to sharing me with house guests."

Izzy raised one eyebrow. It seemed like Great Aunty V was a few sarnies short of a picnic, as Mum would say.

"But to be quite honest, my work keeps me busy. I run Drama classes for local kids in the studio downstairs. Some of them begin the classes hating it, but by the end they all bloom in confidence," Great Aunty V smiled. "I was so excited to hear that you're a prima ballerina!"

Izzy blushed. "Hardly. I've only been taking lessons for a couple of years."

Great Aunty V held her hand to her ear. "Speak up, child! My hearing isn't what it used to be."

"I'm a ballerina," Izzy said louder, sitting up straight. "But I'm quitting soon. The show on Saturday will be my last."

"I see," Great Aunty V said, looking concerned. "What happened?"

Izzy could feel her eyes fill up with tears. She didn't expect to say what she said next, but there was something safe about Great Aunty V. "I completely humiliated myself at the last ballet show. I was about to do my solo piece but then I realised how scary it all was: the big stage, the bright lights. Tonnes of people in the audience. And I...froze."

Great Aunty V nodded, as though prompting Izzy to carry on. So, she did.

"I gawped like a goldfish and ran off stage. And none of the other girls in my ballet class have talked to me since. Including my so-called best friend Lottie," Izzy blurted out. It was the most she'd talked about this to anyone.

Great Aunty V sighed. "Let me ask you something. Do you enjoy ballet?"

Izzy nodded. "Yes. At least, I used to."

"What do you love about it?"

"Oh," Izzy said. No one had ever asked her that. "It's hard to put into words. I guess... When I'm doing normal things like speaking to other kids at school, or putting my hand up to answer a question, I'm so worried about looking silly that my mind goes into overdrive. But when I dance, I don't do any of that. That part of my brain switches off. And I feel free."

Great Aunty V was silent. Izzy felt her cheeks colour. She felt like she'd said too much.

"Then you must stick with it," Great Aunty V said. "Don't ever let fear stop you from being true to yourself."

Easier said than done, Izzy thought.

Great Aunty V hopped down from the dining room chair (she really was very short). "Now that you've eaten, let me give you a tour of the house," she said.

After the tour, Izzy had her theory confirmed: Great Aunty V was loopier than a rollercoaster.

Izzy followed the old lady up several flights of narrow stairs, each one narrower than the last.

"Here's the bathroom. The hot water tap only works if you sing it a nursery rhyme first. Don't ask me why, it's been that way since 1989."

"Here's the study. This room only gets heating on the third Wednesday of the month, so I avoid it from October 'til April. My fingers are too elegant to be frostbitten, thank you very much."

Izzy followed her up the final, and narrowest, staircase into the attic bedroom. It had a fluffy cream carpet and a four-poster bed in the centre of the room. Compared to the yellow living room, it was an oasis of calm.

On the dressing table sat a fancy-looking wooden box

with a ballerina on top. Izzy skipped over to it.

"That's my jewellery box. You're welcome to have a look inside."

Izzy didn't need any further encouragement to open the box. She spotted pearl bracelets and diamond earrings nestled in the satin folds of the jewellery box. She held up a glamorous dangly earring studded with jewels against her ear and looked in the mirror.

Izzy frowned. She saw nothing but a little girl playing dress-up.

Great Aunty V hauled herself up on the bed. "You can try them on, if you like."

"I can't. Mum says I have to wait until Year Seven before I can get my ears pierced."

"In that case, I have some clip-on earrings you can borrow," Great Aunty V winked. "I think they're in the spare room downstairs," she said before leaving the room.

Izzy returned to the jewellery box. And that's when she spotted something that stood out from the rest.

She pulled out a bracelet made from wooden beads and held together by a ratty length of string. It didn't compare to the glittering jewels in the box.

Each bead was painted with a different letter. Izzy

squinted and saw that the letters spelled D-A-H-L-I-A-+-V-E-R-N-I-C-E. She guessed that Vernice was Great Aunty V, but she had no idea who or what Dahlia was.

She slipped the bracelet on. "What the..." Izzy muttered to herself. The wooden beads began to glow and grew warm against her wrist.

Suddenly, she was no longer in Great Aunty V's bedroom.

Later that night Izzy would try to make sense of what happened next. It was the single strangest thing that had ever happened to her.

A series of moving images flicked through Izzy's mind like a slideshow. Izzy was on stage, nailing her performance at the ballet show. Izzy was at school, laughing and joking with her ex-friend Lottie. Izzy was eating dinner with her parents, the pain of Dev's absence lessened.

Weirdest of all, a peculiar feeling surged through her body.

Izzy felt...brave. More than brave. Like she could take on the world.

Suddenly, she was back at the dressing table. Izzy hurriedly removed the bracelet and stuffed it back into the jewellery box. Instantly, the superhero feeling faded.

The next morning Izzy woke up feeling groggy. Her bad dreams about Saturday's ballet show kept her up half the night. But any morning brain-fog quickly disappeared after her ice-cold shower. Bizarrely, Great Aunty V was right: the water warmed up nicely once she sang Twinkle, Twinkle, Little Star.

Izzy sat down at the dining table where a bowl of grey mush was waiting for her. This morning it tasted just like the pancakes with maple syrup Mum had made for her birthday.

"Good morning, Great Aunty V!" Izzy chirped.

Aunty V chuckled. Today she was dressed in a burnt orange blouse with matching wide-legged slacks. She looked like a Halloween pumpkin on legs. "I'm glad you're in a good mood, sweetness. I'll need you to channel that energy in my Drama class today."

Izzy dropped her spoon. "What?"

"You didn't think I'd let your fabulous performance skills go to waste, did you? I'd like you to teach a class for my students. They're so excited to meet you."

Izzy felt like her breakfast would make a return at any second.

"I-I'm not so sure about that," Izzy stammered.

"Being sure about things is overrated," Great Aunty V chuckled. "Now get your leotard on, slow-coach. Winston and I don't like to be late."

*

Izzy, Winston and Great Aunty V didn't need to go far - the drama studio was in the basement. While Great Aunty V answered the door to students and Winston chased a fly, Izzy tried to calm herself down.

She was about to perform in front of complete strangers. They were going to judge her. And there was nowhere to run if she fluffed it.

Not if you fluff it, but when, Izzy told herself. *Because you can't do anything right.*

By 10am sharp the studio was filled with chatting older kids dressed in t-shirts, tracksuit bottoms or leggings. It was clear by the smiles and hugs that they all knew each other. They fussed over Winston, who purred with delight while they rubbed his belly. But no one looked twice at Izzy.

Even the cat gets more notice than you.

Izzy was in a room full of people but had never felt more alone.

Great Aunty V clapped to get everyone's attention. The room fell silent and the twenty or so students sat cross-legged on the floor. Winston jumped onto her back and draped himself across her shoulder like a furry black parrot.

"Today we have a very special guest. This is my great-niece, Isabelle," Great Aunty V pointed to Izzy who sat in the corner. "She's an exceptionally talented ballerina and she will be teaching us some basic moves."

A few of the boys groaned. "But, Miss! Ballet is for girls," one muttered.

"Luke, to practice ballet requires strength, determination and discipline," Great Aunty V said. "I can't think of anyone who wouldn't benefit from that."

Strong. Determined. Disciplined. If Izzy had to describe herself, those three words would be at the bottom of the list.

Great Aunty V did the register then led the warm-up. The other students wriggled their bodies and yelled out silly voices with enthusiasm while Izzy stood in the corner, tummy roiling with nerves. Although she was tall for her age, Izzy was younger than most students here. By the way they talked she realised they were probably all in secondary school.

"Now we're going to play Hot Spot!" Great Aunty V yelled over the chattering students.

The kids immediately formed a giant circle and Izzy followed suit. A couple of girls argued over who would stand in the centre.

"Shanice, you went first last time darlin'," Great Aunty V said. "Zora can start us off today."

The girl called Zora smiled smugly at Shanice, who rolled her eyes before collapsing into giggles. It was clear that they were good friends.

"Zora, you will start singing any song you like, within reason. No bad language in my studio, please. Then someone else will jump in and sing a song that is linked to the first one until everyone has sung."

Everyone. Has. Sung. Izzy couldn't think of more spine-chilling words. Just standing in front of strangers in her silly leotard was bad enough. But to make her sing?

"Take it away, Zora!" Great Aunty V said.

Zora began singing the first few bars of a pop song. Her voice wasn't particularly good but she was enthusiastic and her voice projected beautifully. After a few seconds, another girl jumped forward into the circle and started singing a different song. She even threw in a few cute dance moves while the rest of the circle clapped along.

Izzy ran through potential songs in her head. If she was forced to sing, what would be the least embarrassing option?

Then it hit her. She could recite a poem! Izzy cast her mind back to last term when her Year Five class learned Life Doesn't Frighten Me by a writer called Maya Angelou. She'd at least remember the first verse.

"I want to see some boys join in," Great Aunty V yelled over the clapping.

And they did. They sang, rapped and rhymed during their fifteen seconds or so in the spotlight. They seemed dazzlingly confident and relaxed.

Izzy tried to make herself as small as possible. If she just hung back then no one would notice that—

"Your turn next, babe." The teen girl standing next to Izzy smiled gently and pushed her into the empty space.

The other kid singing slipped back into the circle. All eyes were on Izzy.

The fluorescent lighting felt too harsh, the room too hot, the clapping too loud. She took a deep breath to recite the first line of the poem.

But nothing came out.

It was just like the last ballet show. Izzy wanted to speak but she was frozen solid by her fear. Her mind went blank and she couldn't remember even the first line of the poem.

The only thing she could remember was the last thing she sang this morning.

No WAY. You can't sing that in front of older kids.

"C'mon, sis! You've got this," cheered one of the girls.

Izzy's brown skin flushed beetroot purple. She had no choice. She opened her mouth to sing.

"Twinkle, twinkle, little star / How I wonder what you are," Izzy whispered.

You sang it. Unbelievable.

"Louder!" Great Aunty V shouted.

"Up above the world so high / Like...like...." Her voice cracked.

"Like a diamond in the sky," sang a few other kids. They noticed Izzy was struggling and joined in until the nursery rhyme was over.

They clapped and cheered while Izzy skulked back, her cheeks hot with shame.

"I'm just going to the bathroom," she muttered to Great Aunty V.

"Don't be long, sweetness," she said. "You're demonstrating a few ballet moves for us next."

Izzy wanted to walk out of the front door, into the street and never return. Instead, she ran upstairs. It wasn't until she'd made it to her bedroom that she allowed herself to burst into tears.

Her nightmare had come to life once more. There was no way she'd perform on Saturday, or ever again, without making a total fool of herself.

When was the last time she'd ever felt confident?

Before Dev left home.

Before The Incident at the last ballet show.

Before Lottie stopped talking to her.

But then she remembered what had happened yesterday. The vision she'd had while holding the ratty old bracelet with the wooden beads. It felt like a glimpse into a possible future. And didn't Izzy feel brave when she held the bracelet in her hands? What she wouldn't give to feel that again.

Before she could stop herself, Izzy marched up several flights of stairs until she reached Great Aunty V's bedroom. She flipped open the jewellery box and carefully rummaged around until she found the bracelet.

She cupped it in her palms and closed her eyes. But nothing happened. She didn't have a vision. She didn't suddenly feel confident.

Serves you right for being silly, she thought.

Izzy opened her eyes and slipped the bracelet on over her wrist. The gentle warmth of the beads soothed her. The warmth began to spread.

She gasped as the brown wooden beads glowed amber, emitting a bright light that coursed through her entire body. It felt warm and a little ticklish. That feeling returned: the one where she felt like a superhero. For the first time in ages, she felt excited to perform.

The glowing amber light faded but the flame of courage inside Izzy burned bright. She tucked the bracelet under her sleeve and arranged the jewellery box carefully before heading back to the studio.

Izzy was sure that Great Aunty V wouldn't miss a little old bracelet. But she still looked back to make sure her bedroom looked exactly as she left it.

*

Izzy stood at the front of the studio while the other kids held onto the barre.

"Now, Isabelle is going to teach us some basic ballet moves," Great Aunty V said. "Remember Izzy, they are complete beginners."

"I reckon we can keep up," one boy snickered.

But the unkind comment didn't make Izzy want to crawl into a hole. For the first time, she didn't care what someone else thought.

"We start with position one," she began.

Izzy demonstrated the five basic foot positions of ballet to the rest of the class. In her usual ballet class Izzy couldn't even speak up without her face flushing. But here she was, leading an entire group of teenagers.

This bracelet is epic, she thought.

Classical music piped through the speakers. Izzy span through the basic foot positions faster and faster, way too fast for the rest of the class to keep up. Then she felt the music take over. She abandoned the foot positions and began to dance.

At some point the other kids stopped trying to keep up and looked on in awe. Izzy's dancing took up more space in the centre of the room. She whirled and twirled and did all sorts of things that probably didn't count as ballet but felt good nonetheless.

The rest of the room disappeared. It was just Izzy and the music. She surrendered to it and felt in total control of her body at the same time. For the first time since she could remember, she let go.

After a few minutes the music stopped, and Izzy collapsed into an exhausted heap on the floor. Her chest heaved with exertion. It wasn't the graceful finish that Madame Pirouette taught in her ballet class, but it would have to do.

Great Aunty V burst into a round of applause. The other kids clapped and cheered.

"G'wan, Isabelle!" Some of them yelled.

"Who knew she had it in her," one girl whispered to a friend.

"Of course she had it in her!" Great Aunty V's voice boomed from across the room. "She's my great-niece, after all."

"Miaow!" added Winston. Even he looked impressed.

Izzy jumped up and took a bow, beaming with pride and relief. She could perform after all. She didn't have to be humiliated every time she took the stage.

As long as she had the little wooden bracelet on, everything would be alright.

*

Every morning for the last few weeks, Izzy had woken up with a bad feeling in her tummy. Not the type of bad feeling you get from eating too many fizzy laces. This feeling was more connected to her mind than anything she'd eaten.

Izzy would wake up, remember that the next ballet show wasn't far away and immediately want to hide under the duvet again.

But this morning was different. Izzy felt...nothing. There were no tight knots of anxiety coiling in her tummy. No feelings of dread about tomorrow's ballet show.

She was just a bit peckish.

A gurgling sound came from her belly. Time for breakfast.

"And to think, you were so nervous about doing your performance! Child, you can dance! Just like me when I was younger," Great Aunty V chuckled.

Izzy slurped her bowl of mush, which inexplicably tasted like a Full English fry-up with extra brown sauce. Delish.

After breakfast, Izzy had a lovely hot shower, thanks to her enthusiastic rendition of The Hokey Cokey, and got dressed. Great Aunty V's drama class didn't meet on Fridays so Izzy would have the studio to herself. She was itching to get some rehearsal time in before Pops picked her up that evening.

Just as Izzy stuffed the bracelet into her pocket, she heard a blood-curdling scream.

It was Great Aunty V.

Izzy rushed out of the room and ran upstairs. "I'm coming, Great Aunty V!"

She found her great aunt sitting on her bedroom floor. The contents of her jewellery box were tipped onto the sheepskin rug and her eyes were wet with tears.

"My bracelet...it's gone!" She sniffed. Izzy blinked in shock. "W-what did it look like?" She stuttered.

She hoped Great Aunty V would describe another bracelet entirely. Perhaps one strung with pearls or studded with diamonds. Something actually valuable.

"It's just a little thing. Made from wooden beads. It doesn't look like much but it's the most precious thing I own. I never wear it, but I do like to check to make sure it's there every now and again.

Winston sat beside Great Aunty V, purring forlornly. Why were they this upset over a simple bracelet? *It's not like Great Aunty V needs it,* Izzy thought. *She's so outgoing and confident. Not like me.*

Her anxieties about the ballet show flooded back. It was just one day away. Izzy had to borrow the bracelet for just one day. She would post it back immediately.

Izzy shook her head. "Sorry, Great Aunty V. I haven't seen a bracelet like that." Then she left the room.

*

Izzy avoided Great Aunty V for the rest of the day. She rehearsed in the studio until her solo piece for the ballet show was practically flawless. There was no way she'd run offstage in a panic.

But something nagged at her from the inside. A question

that went unanswered.

Why was Great Aunty V so distraught about a handmade bracelet when she had a box stuffed with real jewels? It didn't make sense.

When Izzy finished her rehearsal, she made her way upstairs to pack her things. But the living room looked different.

Everything was grey. Gone was the ever-present sunshine pouring through the windows that tinted everything lemon-yellow. A chill laced the air.

"Great Aunty V?" Izzy said. There was no response.

She followed the empty hallways until she reached the top of the house. Great Aunty V was still in her bedroom, curled up in bed.

Izzy crept over to her. She was completely still, with a handkerchief in one hand and a piece of paper in the other.

Izzy gasped. "Great Aunty V? Are you still alive?!" she said, shaking her great aunt.

Great Aunty V awoke with a start. The paper in her hand fluttered to the ground. "Of course I'm alive! You think I'm that close to the grave, little girl? Chuh!"

"Sorry," Izzy muttered. She bent down to pick up the paper and hand it back to Great Aunty V. But it wasn't a piece of paper at all. It was an old photograph.

Curiosity got the better of her. Izzy took a closer look.

It showed two young Black women, heads tipped back in laughter. One was very short and the other was a little taller. Judging by the hair and clothes (spherical afros, funny-looking trousers with wide legs), Izzy guessed it was taken a very long time ago.

There were other people milling about in the photo behind them, but the two women didn't pay them any mind. They were in their own tiny universe. When Izzy looked carefully, she could see that they were holding hands.

On the back of the photo were the words 'Dahlia and Vernice, 1978'.

That name again. Dahlia.

"Who's this?" Izzy asked, holding up the photo.

Great Aunty V yawned and sat up. "That's me and my Dahlia," she said. Izzy detected a note of sadness in her voice.

Winston jumped onto the bed and curled up on Great Aunty V's lap.

Izzy placed the photo back down. "Was she a friend, or...?"

"Dahlia Brown was the love of my life," she said frankly.

Izzy blushed. Guilt immediately flooded her.

The bracelet belonged to the love of her life. And Izzy had stolen it.

"The plans that Dahlia and I had! We were going to open a performing arts school together, you know. Then retire back home in Jamaica when the bitter winters got too much for our old bones."

"What happened?" Izzy asked.

"Miaowwww!" Winston purred angrily.

"It's alright, Winston. I can talk about it now," Great Aunty V said. She sighed deeply. "Sadly, my parents had other plans for my future. And those plans didn't involve my Dahlia. They told me it would bring shame upon the family."

Winston rubbed his head gently against Great Aunty V's tummy. If Izzy didn't know any better, she'd think the cat was trying to comfort her.

"By the time I realised that I didn't care what anyone else thought, it was too late. Dahlia Brown had disappeared from my life. Well, not totally disappeared," she sighed.

"The bracelet," Izzy muttered.

"It's my most precious possession," she said. "Dahlia carved the wood, painted the letters and imbued it with her essence. Whenever I feel a little unsure of myself, I wear the bracelet and feel instantly braver."

Great Aunty V's eyes grew watery with tears and Izzy felt

something break inside of her. "And now I've lost it," she muttered.

"No, you haven't lost it. I took it," Izzy blurted out.

She told Great Aunty V everything: the vision she had when she first held the bracelet. The superhuman confidence boost it gave her. And how she couldn't dance without it.

Izzy took the bracelet from her pocket and stuffed it into Great Aunty V's palm. "I was going to post it back straight after my ballet show. I promise!"

Winston hissed.

"Oh, Izzy. You didn't have to lie about it!" Great Aunty V said.

Izzy sniffed, trying to hold back tears. "Would you have let me borrow it if I asked?"

Great Aunty V shook her head. "No, darlin'. But only because I know you don't need it. If you rely on the bracelet, you'll never grow into the person I know you can be."

"But if I dance without it...I might fail," Izzy said. There it was: her worst fear out in the open.

Great Aunty V shrugged. "Better to try and fail then to never have tried at all, is what I say."

Izzy nodded. "Dahlia must've been a very special person," she said. "The bracelet made me feel invincible. It felt like every one of my problems disappeared."

Great Aunty V smiled. "Yes. Dahlia could have that effect on you."

"What's she up to now?" Izzy asked.

"I have no idea. We fell out of contact many years ago."

"You know, Great Aunty V," Izzy began. "I bet we could find Dahlia on Facebook."

"Face-what?"

"You've never heard of Facebook? I thought old people loved it!"

Great Aunty V shifted on the edge of the bed. "I already told you, Isabelle. Me and technology don't get along. It's all so complicated," she sighed. "And once you master one device, they go and change all the buttons so you have to start from scratch!"

Izzy narrowed her eyes. "If I didn't know any better, I'd say you were afraid."

"No, not afraid. Just...set in my ways, I suppose."

Izzy pulled out her phone. "It's not hard at all. Trust me. I can show you, if you want?"

"I'm not sure about this, Izzy. What if she doesn't reply?"

Izzy shrugged. "Better to try and fail then to never have tried at all."

Great Aunty V hesitated before reaching her hand out for the phone.

*

Izzy took deep breaths to calm herself, inhaling the faint fumes of hair spray that lingered backstage. She closed her eyes and let the chaotic energy wash over her. She heard Madame Pirouette making last-minute adjustments to tutus and fairy wings, and the excited chatter of the other dancers as they limbered up.

The sound of applause punctured her thoughts. Izzy opened her eyes. She was up next.

“Sugar Plum Fairies, assume your positions!” Madame Pirouette yelled.

She and other dancers fluttered to the stage wings. Izzy’s heart was racing. Why did everyone else seem so calm and relaxed? Her hand flew to her wrist, where the bracelet used to be.

The first few bars of music began to play. A lovely warm feeling filled Izzy, like stepping into a hot bath. The butterflies in her tummy eased up. She stepped on stage to do the thing she loved more than anything else: dance.

AMELIA ST CLAIR AND THE LONG-ARMED KILLER

JOSEPH COELHO

ILLUSTRATED BY SELOM SUNU

CHAPTER 1: ABOARD THE NEPTUNE'S PRONG

Going on a cruise is great the first time, but me and my squirt of a brother Tobias have been on loads. Dad loves them, always telling me "it's the only way to travel Amelia". We've cruised around the Bintan islands, sunbathed around the Bahamas, watched dolphins in the Indian Ocean and fished around the Caribbean. Sounds great, but once you've done one cruise you've done them all; it's all swimming pools (which Tobias loves) and sun loungers (which Mum lives on) and buffet bars (that Dad hogs). Sure, you get to travel the world, but all you see of each country are the ports, filled with tourist junk. I've lost count of the magnets and keychains I've collected from all our cruises.

Oh yeah, and on top of all of that you get stuck on a boat with your annoying little brother, who's eight but thinks he's twelve, and who finds it funny to drop water bombs on you when you're trying to read on deck or to tell Felix that you like him. Felix is on holiday here with his parents too (okay, I admit he is kinda cute, but I don't like him, like him! Not like that... yuck!).

So here we are, on yet another cruise, this time around the Similan Islands, off the coast of Thailand. Passing white beaches, cruising over turquoise waters, yes, yes all very picturesque, but god I'm bored. I wish something exciting would happen....

*

"Sarafina, try this delicious new octopus dish," says Dad to Mum, as he waddles to our sun loungers with several plates fresh from the buffet.

"The food isn't going anywhere Ralph, you don't have to eat

it all now," says Mum, looking like a goddess on her lounger, wrapped in a sarong. I take after Mum the most: we both have a huge pile of books by our loungers. At the top of my pile is a book all about Anansi - a trickster god who always wins.

Tobias runs over to snatch some cakes from one of Dad's plates, in his shorts and T-shirt and smiling so the whole world can see the gap where one of his milk teeth have come out. "Your boyfriend is over there!" he says, pointing to the other side of the boat where Felix is taking photos of the island Koh Tachai.

"Shut up!" I tell him, which gets me a stern look from Mum. Felix is pointing his camera straight down. Normally when someone does that there are dolphins or flying fish flashing their silver in the ships wake, so I get up to join him.

"Going to see your BOOOOY friend," chants Tobias.

"I WILL kill you!" I snap, before Mum raises her finger. "Sorry Mummy," I say. I check my fro, make sure my headband is still tight and head over to Felix.

"Whatcha photographing?"

"Oh, hey Amelia, look! We've got new passengers," Felix adjusts his glasses and gives me his serious look. I look over the side, which I don't like doing because I always forget that this cruise ship, the Neptune's Prong, is five stories high. Way below us a smaller boat has docked, and its crew are being brought onboard along with their equipment. "It's a science vessel. They got in trouble last night and our ship rescued them, they've been unpacking their equipment all morning," says Felix, snapping away as the science crew struggle with a huge wooden box.

"How do you know all this?"

"Craig told me."

Craig is the Captain's son. He's thirteen like me and Felix but is a bit shy. He only really talks to Felix because they're both mad about the Crafts Club, where they can be found most days building stuff. Craig's alright I guess, but when he does talk, he always reminds us that his dad is the Captain.

Felix starts zooming in on his camera, he always has that thing hanging around his neck. "Oh boy!" says Felix zooming in. I'm staring, but I can't make out what's so shocking.

"Let me see!" I snatch the camera (but, you know, in a nice way) and peer down at the boat. The crew are struggling with a huge wooden box that says FRAGILE in big letters and THIS WAY UP. A tall lean man with a scraggly salt and pepper beard wearing cargo pants (that should never be worn) and greying dreads in a single thick plait down his back, is barking orders at the staff.

"That's Dr Graveller the lead scientist! Craig said they made a new discovery on the sea floor."

"He doesn't seem very nice the way he is shouting!" I whisper as the camera tries to focus. It does and I gasp: Dr Graveller is looking straight up at me and it feels like slushed ice is pouring into my stomach.

CHAPTER 2: A SONG AND A DANCE

It's evening and we're in the Diner's Lounge listening to Big Ronny, the ship's cheesy singer in his silver sequined jacket (honestly, I'm not kidding... it's a silver sequined jacket!). There are three backing dancers all in ridiculous feathery outfits. Tobias doesn't care. He dives into his tech-sack; that's the stupid name he's given to the rucksack containing all his gadgets for playing games, taking action shots, reading his eBooks, his phone and of course his drone. He fishes out his stupid game machine and is immediately told by Mum to turn the volume down.

Dad is making constant trips to the buffet bar, annoying Mum every five seconds with "Sarafina you should try this." I'm trying to read about how Anansi trapped a bunch of hornets in a jar, but now the singer is ruining Beyoncé's

'Single Ladies' and trying to get us to lift our hands up. Thankfully I spy Felix in the corner with Craig.

"What are you guys doing?" I ask. Craig looks scared. I mean he often looks scared (Mum thinks he's 'just a lovely shy boy') but this is a different type of scared. "What's wrong?"

Felix grabs me and bundles us both through a door into the stairwell. He turns to stare through the glass door at Ronny in his glitter-ball vomit jacket. "Craig just told me that Big Ronny is a convicted criminal."

"Really?!" I am desperate for gossip.

"Tell her Craig." Craig shuffles his feet. "It's okay Craig, you can trust Amelia."

Craig looks up at me from under his twists. "My Dad, the Captain, got left a strange note on pink paper saying that Big Ronny is wanted for tax evasion. Dad had to sack him. This is his last performance."

"Oooh a strange note! This is a mystery waiting to be solved," I say, as I remember the first time I heard about Anansi the spider from my grandmother, on one of our trips to Jamaica and how she described him as being able to solve any problem.

"I'll miss his singing," says Felix, as Ronny's shouts of "PUT YOUR HANDS UUUP!" boom through the stairwell door.

"But he's terrible, I feel sorry for the dancers, they'll have no one to perform with. They're the main reason Mum makes us come every evening."

"Well, my Dad, the Captain, has already got a new singer. Roxy Ravenscroft, she's brilliant, she has an amazing voice. She's a passenger on the ship but she offered to sing, every night. There she is." Craig points through the window at a lady sitting in the audience. She has a mass of auburn tinted curly hair that makes me think of autumn leaves. But what really strikes me is how still she is; whilst everyone else is laughing and throwing their hands up, Roxy is just glaring. Maybe she hates Big Ronny's singing just as much as me.

A door slams open on the floor beneath us. We creep to the bannister and look down. It's Dr Graveller. He has shaved and changed his clothes and looks far less dishevelled than before. He pins another scientist up against the wall (this one is much shorter and bald).

"That's his assistant Dr Nathan." Whispers Felix.

"What have I told you? Nothing can interfere with our work," growls Dr Graveller.

"But I don't know where it is!" Dr Nathan is looking down, reminding me of the way Tobias acts when he's in trouble. "We should tell the Captain."

"No, no one can know. This is our discovery and ours

alone. If you tell anyone, you can forget your career, you can kiss your life goodbye." And with that, Dr Graveller storms away, leaving the little bald Dr Nathan to wipe sweat from his forehead as he disappears down the steps. "What was all that about?" says Felix. I notice that the whole time he has had his camera in his hands. "Were you taking pictures?"

"Better than that! I recorded them."

"Brilliant. What do you think they were talking about?" I ask.

"My dad, the Captain, has given the scientists a room on the engine deck. Maybe they were talking about something from there?" suggests Craig.

"What are you guys doing back here?" shouts Tobias, as he bundles into the stairwell from the Diner's Lounge. "Mum wants you Amelia."

"Let's meet tomorrow by the pool, this definitely requires more investigation," I tell the others, before heading back into the Lounge to listen to Big Ronny ruin Rihanna's "Umbrella".

CHAPTER 3: A STRANGULATION!

The following day, we're all at the pool. We play sharks, which is basically like tag in the water, but I make everyone call it crocodiles because Anansi once tricked a crocodile and then spent the rest of his life running over water to avoid being snapped. The sun is shining, and everything is great… until we hear a scream.

A horrible scream that comes from the portside (that's the left side of the boat as Dad keeps reminding me). People rush out of the pool to see what's happening. Mum and Dad join them.

Dad still has an octopus tentacle in his mouth (he can't get enough of the seafood buffet) and is yelling, "Stand back, we're doctors!" Dad is a top surgeon and Mum is an anaesthetist.

Mum and Dad rush ahead pushing through the crowd to get to a man laying on the floor.

"Stand back everyone," says Mum, "give him room."

A silence has fallen over the crowd, the man isn't moving.

Dad bends down and feels his neck.

Felix bends down to whisper to me. "Do you recognise him? It's the bald scientist, Dr Nathan from last night." I don't want to look, but curiosity gets the better of me. Felix is right, it's him.

"Get the captain!" Dad shouts out. "This man has been murdered by strangulation."

"Where will they put the body?" asks Tobias, as the crowd leaves and the staff rope off the area.

"It will go into the morgue," says Craig, who is chewing nervously on a sugared lace.

"They don't have morgues on ships," I say.

"They do, and prison cells." Craig says, almost too enthusiastically. "My Dad, the captain, has taken me around the whole ship. There is a morgue right at the bottom, in case people die and there is a prison cell for criminals."

"Makes sense," says Felix. "These cruise ships are full of really old people, someone is bound to... you know... kick the bucket! Do you think that Dr Nathan was killed by Dr Graveller?" he asks us.

I nod. I've had the same thought. "Maybe we should tell someone what we heard," I say, taking one of the sugar laces from Craig's heaving bag.

"I dunno, it's not much to go on and it's a pretty serious accusation," says Felix. He's probably right, it was just an argument, surely a world-renowned scientist (according to Craig) would not be going around strangling people.

"Best to forget about it," I say, mainly because I want to keep thinking about it and I can't think straight with everyone talking all at once. This is turning into a proper mystery, and just like Anansi I'm going to use my cunning to get to the bottom of it. "Let's go on the skybikes to clear our heads, I haven't been on those yet."

The skybikes are a bit like a rollercoaster, with plastic egg-shaped carriages that hang from a track that goes all around the ship, except they use pedal power. I've been putting off going on them because I'm not mad on heights, but this seems like the perfect time. It will give me some alone thinking time. Normally we have to queue but, with the Captain's son with us, we jump right to the front. I don't know why the staff are so scared of the Captain, I've met Craig's Dad loads and he's super nice. Him and Dad get along like two boring old farts. They're both from St Elizabeth in Jamaica, and whenever they get together they spend ages saying 'do you know so and so...' and they go on and on and on.

We head up the stairs to the launchpad (or at least that's what it's called, it's really just a platform at the top of some metal stairs where you can clamber into an skybike, they really should just call it a platform, cos that's what it is!).

The staff strap us in. I take some deep breaths and tell myself to just enjoy the ride. At first, it's really cool. Tobias is in the skybike in front of me whopping and cheering,

Felix and Craig are on the track next to ours so we can ride side by side and shout at each other.

There are loads of things to look at, as the track takes us through the amusement park, past the merry-go-round and over the tops of the hotdog stands. It's so easy to forget that we are in the middle of the ocean. But then the track leaves the amusement park and follows the side of the ship. This bit I don't like, because from this height it's like you're cycling over the water.

"This is amazing!" hoots Tobias, as he speeds towards a downward dip in the track. I swallow hard and just keep going. I don't want to throw up and if I look at the undulating waves, I might just do that. That's when someone catches my eye.

Down below I spy Dr Graveller in a white anorak, like the kind that the staff wear, as if he's in disguise, but his ornate plait hanging down his back is a huge giveaway.

"Felix, look it's him!" I say, as Felix comes up beside me. Dr Graveller is looking shifty. Even from this height it is easy to see that he's trying to be incognito as he keeps looking backwards himself like he's 'up to no good', as Mum says whenever she sees Tobias planning an oh-so-funny practical joke. Felix and I slow down, as Craig and Tobias speed on unaware that they may have just passed over the head of a murderer! (Well, probably).

We follow Dr Graveller as he makes his way along the starboard side of the boat, quietly, trying not to be seen. Luckily, this side of the ship has loads of large orange lifeboats attached to cranes, ready to be dropped over the side, they're totally self-contained more like little submarines than boats, (to keep passengers dry in emergencies I guess). They're big enough for us to peep over and peer down without being seen.

Dr Graveller comes to a door and taps on it three times. It is answered by a member of the ship's kitchen staff dressed in white with a little chef's hat. The staff member disappears inside the ship and comes back moments later with a plate of octopus tentacles, just like the ones Dad was eating earlier from the seafood buffet. Dr Graveller takes them and rushes off down the boat so fast that we struggle to keep up on the skybikes high above him. We follow him until he disappears inside the ship.

"Oh man!" I say, frustrated that these ridiculous bikes are stuck to a track.

"Don't worry," says Felix, "At least we've learnt one thing."

"What's that?"

"That Dr Graveller does not want to be seen."

CHAPTER 4: A FEATHERY REVEAL

It's evening, and we're back in the Diner's Lounge listening to Big Ronny totally slaughter my favourite songs, as we try to figure out a way to prove that Dr Graveller is the murderer. I have been cycling through Felix's camera footage again and again.

"What's the point of all this filming if you don't film anything interesting?"

"It's an art form, I'm finding my visual voice," says Felix. "One day I'll film something spectacular, but that can't happen unless I practice."

"Well, your visual voice sounds boring," I tell him, and we both crack up.

"OOOoooh Felix and Amelia sitting in a tree…K.I.S.S…" I prod Tobias hard in the arm to shut him up (not really hard, just big sister hard). "Why is shoddy Ronny still singing? I thought you said he was a criminal."

"Dad said it was a misunderstanding," says Craig, with a gobstopper stuffed into the side of his cheek. He really is speaking up more, which is nice. "He sorted it all out with Dad, he was in some trouble but it was years ago so Dad said he could stay."

"Oh great," I say. "So that's two more weeks of him ruining every song ever written". As if on cuc Ronny finishes his set and says:

"Thank you, ladies and gentlemen, me and The Flighty Flamingo Dancers will be right back after this short break." People actually clap, and one person even cheers… oh god, it's Mum! Then I spy Roxy, in the same seat as last night, glaring, her arms crossed.

"Hey, do you think it was Roxy who sent that letter to the captain, to get Ronny fired and take his job?" I say, my cunning Anansi mind connecting threads (or should I say… webs!).

"Oh wow, I bet it was," says Tobias. We watch as Big Ronny heads to the buffet bar, helps himself to a plate of the Seafood Special, and then goes out on deck.

"How can he eat in-between songs?" I say, shaking my head. "He'll be spraying us with bits of seafood all night."

"Look at this." Tobias has been hunched over his tablet this whole time. He shows us a website showing a smiling Dr Graveller on a boat. It's from an article in one of those science magazines. "Says here that Dr Graveller and his team have been exploring the ocean's depths, uncovering its secrets from new species to lost treasures. Last year, his team found the wreck of the HMS Fortitude that had twenty billion pounds worth of gold bullion!" Tobias' eyes widen at that as he flicks through the article, showing us photos of Dr Graveller opening crates filled with gold.

"He must be rich!" says Craig.

"Nope," says Tobias, "all the gold had to go to the Brazilian government who funded the expedition."

"That explains it!" I say. "The reason why he wanted the bald guy, I mean Dr Nathan to not talk about their discovery. Maybe he strangled Dr Nathan to keep him silent." I'm almost giddy as I can see the web of clues taking shape. Nana always said I was a "wily one" better than even Anansi and I think she might be right.

"I don't know," says Felix, "seems pretty extreme to kill a member of your scientific team."

"Money makes people do crazy things," whispers Craig, as he replaces his gobstopper with a jelly cola bottle. I don't care what Felix says, I have good instincts about people and Dr Graveller has DODGE written all over him. Besides, in my notebook I've already decided he is the murderer.

"What does your Dad think, Craig? Has he said who he thinks did it?"

"Dad says that at sea there are no police, it's all down to the Captain and he can't do anything if there are no suspects."

"That settles it then," I say, "we have to find the murderer."

The Flighty Flamingo Dancers are back on stage doing the same routine they do every night. The dance ends with them making a big pink fan, and Big Ronny "magically" appears from behind them whilst a fountain squirts behind him. They are working up to the big reveal and Felix has his camera out.

"I love this number," he says zooming in. The dancers have got into formation making the big pink fan, parting one at a time to the beat of a drum whilst singing....

"Ronny is the man,
who musically can,
he sings and he dings,
like a big brass band."

(Yes, it is that cheesy!) And then they reveal Big Ronny, but he doesn't look right. He's just standing there in that sparkly suit (which is just wrong at the best of times), he's not even holding the microphone to his mouth. He is just staring and gasping, bits of gourmet fish fingers spraying from his mouth, and then he falls flat on to his face. People gasp and scream... all except Roxy, she is nowhere to be seen.

CHAPTER 5: LOCKDOWN

The boat is on lockdown. Thankfully Big Ronny is not dead, but he is in a coma. Someone tried to strangle him too but they didn't get to finish the job, Dad says Big Ronny passed out from the strangling and then banged his head when he fell onto the stage. But it's a mystery how no one saw who did it. Now, everyone must stay in their cabins except to pick up food until the murderer has been found. Mum and Dad are scared, they keep checking in on Tobias and me to make sure we're okay. And to try to get us to talk about our feelings. So, when Craig invites us to join him and Felix in his super luxury apartment, we can't wait to go.

"No way!" says Mum.

"It'll be fine," says Dad, "the Captain's quarters are the safest place on the ship."

Mum relents but insists on walking us up to Craig's cabin 'just in case.' Being inside isn't too bad as the weather is grey outside, but it is scary to think that a murderer is loose on the ship. I'm still convinced it is Dr Graveller, but why would he kill Big Ronny?

Once Mum leaves us at Craig's cabin, I snatch Felix's camera.

"Hey" he says, "I've already checked it a hundred times, there are no clues."

"Ronny must have been strangled backstage as he waited for his big reveal, but why didn't the murderer finish the job?" I scroll through his footage, because no one else has my detective skills. It's horrible seeing it all play out again; the confused look on Ronny's face before he falls down, the screams of the dancers. I rewind the film and play it again, this time trying to spot when Roxy leaves her seat. She is prime suspect number 2 in my book.

"What if Roxy killed Ronny to take his place on the stage? She was all set to be the star of the ship if Ronny hadn't worked things out with Craig's Dad." I say, twirling a loose curl on my finger.

"If Roxy did this, does that mean she killed the bald guy too?" says Tobias. I have to say, I'm a little impressed with how my annoying little brother is getting the hang of the art of detection.

"It can't be Roxy," says Felix, diving into his camera bag to change a lens. "She has no reason to kill Dr Nathan." He has a point, and the video confirms it. I spot Roxy speaking to some people on another table, as the camera pans to the stage for Ronny's final curtain call. But then something else catches my eye.

"What have you seen?" asks Felix.

"Look behind Ronny! When he falls down, there is something glistening and moving in the background lights but it's hard to make out."

"I don't know, looks like it's just reflections from a wet floor to me. We are on a ship, things do get wet," says Felix.

"That's not it." I say, "and the floor was wet when the bald guy got killed, so even if it is just that it's still a clue." They all look confused.

"Maybe they wet themselves," says Tobias. "That does happen I saw it on a documentary, people poop and wee when they die."

"Errrrrr and NO!" I say. "That's not it, this might be a hint at how the murderer is getting to the victims without being seen." Everyone still looks confused. "We're on a ship, right? So, what if Dr Graveller is using diving gear to get to his victims, maybe he swims around the ship to where he'll know they'll be, climbs up the side of the ship with... erm... grappling hooks, murders his victim then jumps overboard and swims to another part of the ship unseen."

Now they are all staring at me like I'm crazy. I guess when I say it out loud it does sound a little far-fetched.

"That could be it," says Craig, surprising us all. "Dr Graveller is a deep-sea scientist and explorer, he would have all the diving gear and maybe even climbing equipment. The floor could be wet from his dripping diving gear."

"Exactly!" I exclaim. "Thank you, Craig!" and I take one of his tangy sweets to celebrate.

"Okay, but that doesn't tell us why." Again, Felix has a point and I almost hate him for it. "We know why he might have killed Dr Nathan, but he had no reason to kill Ronny."

"And that's why we have to investigate!"

*

I was expecting far more resistance to my plan to break into Dr Graveller's lab to look for clues, but I think after spending hours in lockdown everyone's up for just about anything.

With Craig's dad on the ship's bridge, we are adult-free to make our plans. Craig runs off to his dad's bedroom and comes back moments later with a key. "This is the ship skeleton key; it opens every door onboard. We can definitely get into Dr Graveller's lab with this."

"Well done, Craig!" I say. "I didn't know you had it in you." Craig smiles sheepishly as he grabs a packet of sweets from the table. The ship-wide tannoy crackles into life.

Hello, ladies and gentlemen, this is your Captain speaking. I have received reports of some slightly bumpy weather up ahead so do take care when moving around your cabins.

"Oh no," says Craig.

"What?" we all say in unison.

"When Dad says 'bumpy weather', what he actually means is a storm."

*

The ship feels deserted as we walk down the silent corridors and take the empty staircases down into the belly of the ship. At the Diner's Lounge we hear voices. We peek inside to see a smattering of people collecting meals to take back to their cabins, but, on a far table, breaking thc rules, are Roxy Ravenscroft and Dr Graveller. She has her hands in his and they are looking longingly into each other's eyes like... errrrr! Like boyfriend and girlfriend!

"Oh my god guys, look!" I say, "Dr Graveller and Roxy Ravenscroft are like together... like, romantically."

"Errr, nasty!" says Tobias, and for once I agree with him.

"Do you think this means Dr Graveller killed Big Ronny for Roxy, so that she could replace him as the ship's singer?" asks Felix, as he snaps the pair feeding chicken nuggets to each other.

"Yes Felix, brilliant! That must be it, but we need proof and Dr Graveller's lab will be the best place to look."

Using the skeleton key, we get to the engineering deck, where there are pipes and wires running off in all different directions.

"This is where the magic happens," says Craig, "where the engine is kept in working order and where all the sewage gets recycled."

"Oooh can we see that?" asks Tobias.

"No" I say, "we have to stay focused and find the doctor's lab!"

We get halfway down the corridor when we hear voices.

"Quick, in here," Felix bundles us into the nearest room. It's cold and dark.

"Who is it?" says Tobias, as the voices get nearer.

"It's just the maintenance staff," whispers Craig, "but they mustn't see us down here or my dad will kill us."

The pair keep talking as their footsteps fade down the corridor.

"Hey guys where are we? Feels like there are freezer doors on this wall," says Tobias, and I can hear him tugging at something.

"It might be where they keep the ice-cream, we get through 700 pounds of ice-cream a week on this ship." Craig throws the light switch on.

The room is silver, and one wall has three massive horizontal freezer doors along it.

"Help me open this freezer," says Tobias as he struggles to open the door. Craig rushes over and together they heave against the handle. There's a clunk and a mist of frosty air wafts out of the freezer. Tobias and Craig peer through it, hungry for ice-cream only to be met with the frozen body of the dead Dr Nathan!

We scream and run out of the room. "See, I told you the ship has a morgue," breathes Craig as we rush off down the corridor.

"You said it would be ice-cream!" says Tobias. "That wasn't ice-cream!"

"Sorry," says Craig, "but look this must be the lab." He flips out the skeleton key and opens another heavy metal door. The lab has a huge metal table in the middle, facing two massive water tanks bubbling with sea green water. Wooden crates lay open and unpacked on the floor. There are microscopes and books and maps of the seafloor; one with a large 'X' marked in red.

"What do you think he's working on?" asks Felix, snapping photos of the large crates.

"That red cross must show where he found his treasure," says Tobias, eyeing the maps.

"There must be something here that tells us what he's hiding," I say, and then we hear a new voice from behind us...

"I could tell you, but then I'd have to kill you."

We turn to see Dr Graveller in the doorway. His plait of locks hangs over his shoulder and he is wearing ridiculous round green goggles. A smile creeps across his face, as he closes the door and strides towards us with a long hook-ended stick.

CHAPTER 6: INTO THE BELLY

"Please don't kill us!" I shout, as Dr Graveller approaches with his weird green goggles on looking like some mad scientist.

"Kill you! What do you think I am?! I need your help."

"It's a trick!" I yell. "Look he has a weapon!" I point at the long hook-ended stick.

"This is not for you, it's for the monster."

"Monster? Where?" screams Tobias, as Felix spins around with his camera ready to snap the photograph of the century. The ship gives a violent lurch to the side, sending us sprawling to the floor, the ship's tannoy crackling into life.

Ladies and gentlemen, this is your Captain speaking. Nothing to worry about, we are just entering a bit of blustery weather, please stay in your cabins and take care.

"Oh no," says Craig. "When Dad says blustery weather what he actually means is typhoon!" And as if on cue, a massive roll of thunder is heard from outside.

"Oh no, this is bad," says Dr Graveller. "Look kids, we don't have time, I know you've been on my trail like I've been on the monster's. We can help each other, what do you think?"

"We think you murdered your colleague to keep your discovery down here secret and then you tried to kill Big Ronny to make Roxy the star singer because you love her." As I shout, Felix, Tobias and Craig bunch up beside me with make-shift weapons; Tobias with a heavy torch, Craig struggling with a fire hydrant, and Felix holding his camera in a slightly more menacing manner.

"Ha! You're quite the detective. Roxy is indeed a special friend, but I was merely comforting her after the loss of her dear friend Ronny. She was a huge fan, and it was terrible what he went through after he almost got fired, she hates those dancers for ratting him out." We all look at each other realising how wrong we've been. "You're right about one thing though, I do want to keep my discovery secret. But that's going to be hard, given that my discovery is the murderer." We all gasp.

"Your discovery is the murderer?? What do you mean?!" I shout.

Dr Graveller opens up a laptop on the table and spins it round to face us. "Me and my colleague, the poor late Dr Nathan have been exploring the floor of the Andaman Sea. We discovered some incredible structures where the Sunda and Burma tectonic plates meet, truly unique structures that had been built by some intelligent force."

Dr Graveller plays a video of submarine rover footage, just like the stuff you see on telly, weird fish swimming quickly through the bright white light of the rover as it glides deeper into the inky blue sea. Suddenly, the frame fills with what looks like a mound of crab shells, but, as the rover gets nearer, it's clear that the shells have been arranged. They've been used like building bricks to form huge, spiralling structures with regular oval openings winding around them, like buildings, and inside, huge round eyes are glinting in the rover's head lights.

"What are those things?" asks Felix

"Those 'things' are my discovery! I call them Gravelleroctopus Mimicus, or Gravellerpus for short, a species of never-seen-before, highly intelligent octopuses. They are problem solvers and tool users," says Dr Graveller.

Dr Graveller clicks on to another video showing two huge tanks on board a boat. The camera zooms into the dark water of the first tank when, all of a sudden, a huge tentacle smacks onto the glass and rolls across it showing suckers the size of tennis balls. Instead of a tip, this tentacle has a fleshy tentacle-fingered hand!

We all turn terrified to the tanks in the room, the same tanks from the video. Felix walks slowly up to the nearest one, his camera shaking, as we all watch holding our breaths. He gets right up to the glass, and is about to tap on it, when the ship gives another lurch. We all scream.

Dr Graveller laughs, "I said my discovery is the murderer, so it's loose, no longer in the tank."

"But you have two tanks, are there two octopuses, I mean, Gravellerpuses loose?" asks Felix, putting the lens cap firmly onto his camera.

"There were two when we were rescued. But when the specimens were brought on board this vessel, the first of the two Gravellerpuses escaped..."

An alarm goes off, followed by the tannoy crackling into life and the voice of the captain:

Ladies and gentlemen, we are getting reports of water entering the ship, not to worry it's just the rain but please stay in your cabins.

"Water? We saw water at the crime scenes for the bald guy, sorry I mean Dr Nathan, and Ronny," I say.

"Clever detective," says Dr Graveller. "The Gravellerpus needs water, is never far from it in fact, and leaves a wet trail wherever it goes, it likes the dark also, so keeps to the shadows, that's why it didn't finish off big Ronny the stage lights must have scared it off when the dancers revealed him, but if water is leaking onto the ship it could go almost anywhere."

Dr Graveller dives into one of the wooden crates and pulls out four pairs of round goggles with green glass lenses, just like his. "Wear these. Like all octopuses, the Gravellerpus can camouflage so well that it is almost invisible. These glasses will help you see it, they're calibrated to react to the chromatophores in the Gravellerpus's skin."

"Of course!" I yell. "In Felix's video we saw a strange warping of the light when Ronny passed out."

"What you most likely saw was the Gravellerpus moving under camouflage, it really is quite astounding." As he talks, Dr Graveller gives us each a stick.

"Erm, what are we supposed to do with a stick?" I ask.

"It's for protection, the Gravellerpus is a predator that works unseen so it's not used to its prey fighting back, a bonk on its head should be enough to keep you safe. We have to hurry, it could be anywhere." The doctor runs, and we follow with our green goggles in place and sticks in hand. We leave the engineering deck and all immediately slip on the floor; there is water cascading down the steps.

"Are we sinking?" asks Tobias.

"No, don't worry, it always looks worse than it is," says Craig. "It's just the storm water getting in through the doors, Dad says this ship is unsinkable."

"That's what they said about the Titanic!" says Felix, snapping away.

"So, how are we going to find this Gravellerpus?" I ask Dr Graveller. He turns and smiles at me.

"With this." From his pocket he takes out a plastic bag filled with food, and I recognise the octopus tentacles from the Chef's Special Seafood buffet.

"We saw you collect those from the kitchen staff the other day!"

"I thought I was being watched that day." He grins.

"Does the Gravellerpus like seafood?"

"Not exactly, but she will be attracted to it. Remember I said that the first Gravellerpus went missing when we bordered the ship... I'm afraid it found its way into the kitchen and, well, the chef must have mistaken it for one of his ingredients. He cooked it without knowing what it was, but it did make a rather fine Seafood Special, once I did a DNA test of this sample I knew there was only one Gravellerpus to worry about."

"Oh yuck! It was cooked!" says Tobias.

"Afraid so, it was a male, they are far more docile than the females and much smaller, but very tasty. This male happened to be the mate of our second specimen, and she wasn't too happy about people eating her partner. I noticed a pattern after poor Doctor Nathan was killed; he was very partial to the seafood buffet and he had had second helpings. Well, the female Gravellerpus must have smelt her mate on his breath because that was the night she escaped, and he was her first victim."

"That makes total sense," I say, punching the air, "the night Big Ronny was attacked we saw him eat from the buffet car."

"The female Gravellerpus has an extraordinary sense of smell, she will seek out anyone who ate her mate, and she will kill them."

"Oh no, Amelia!" Tobias is grabbing my arm.

"What's wrong Tobias?"

"Who's been eating lots from the seafood buffet?" My stomach feels like it is filling with wet sand as I realise who Tobias means.

"Doctor Graveller, you have to come with us, we think we know where the Gravellerpus will strike next! She's going to try and kill our dad!"

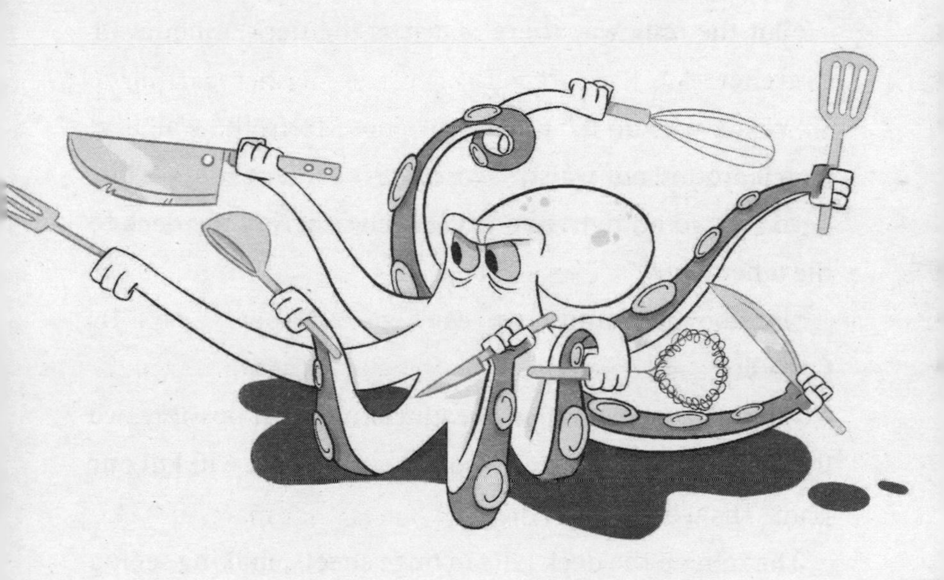

CHAPTER 7: SHIP IN A STORM

We run up the waterfall stairs, taking two at a time. Slipping and sliding as we go, thunder booms around the ship. There is a lurch as a wave hits, sending us sliding down the corridor towards The Diner's Lounge. There is a crash as several vending machines fall over, blocking our way, chocolate bars and sweets roll over the wet floor.

"We can't get to the stairs, we'll have to go round to the other staircase," shouts Felix, whilst pulling Craig back from the spilled sweets.

"But the only way there is across the deck!" shouts Dr Graveller.

"We have to do it." I pull a fire hose from the wall and loop it around our waists. "We haven't got far to go; we just need to hold on tight and get ourselves across the deck to the other lobby."

"It's too dangerous, we can't go out there," says Dr Graveller.

"Your Gravellerpus has already claimed one possibly two lives, we're the only ones who can stop it or it will kill our Dad!" That seems to do the trick.

The rain on the deck falls in huge sheets, making seeing anything through the googles impossible, so we pull them down around our necks. With every lurch of the ship, water streams over the side rails. A huge flash of lightning strikes the skybike track above our heads. It makes a huge groan as it snaps and lands heavily onto one of the orange lifeboats underneath causing its little porthole windows to fly open. The deck looks battered, the sun-loungers in disarray and pool floats all over the floor. The lobby is up ahead. We inch on as lightning turns the sky into a camera-flash-cloud-soup.

I'm reaching for the lobby door, but every time I go to grab the handle Felix tugs me back on the hose. I try again and he yanks me back. I turn to tell him to stop, but the space between me and Felix looks weird, like the light is warping. There is a shimmering by my side, like I'm looking through clear jelly. The jelly ripples as colours swirl from black to purple to luminous green as the Gravellerpus materialises between me and Felix, rippling out of its camouflage with golden bulbous eyes. It's big, far taller than Dad, and is using four of its tentacles as legs. The rest of its tentacles wrap around Felix, Tobias, Craig and me, it's weird tentacle-fingered hands holding each of us tight. I hear Doctor Graveller grunt as he falls down on the deck.

"Use your sticks" he yells. I see Tobias swing his stick towards the Gravellerpus – I've never been so proud of my little brother and completely terrified for him. The Gravellerpus flips back a fleshy fringe where all its tentacles meet, revealing a huge orange beak that snaps out, cracking Tobias' weapon like a matchstick.

Doctor Graveller manages to stand. He takes the bag of Seafood Special (cooked Gravellerpus remains!) from his pocket and waves it at the female. She lets out a sound like a screaming horse, like a cornered rat, like the ocean yelling, and goes for Dr Graveller, tentacles whipping out left and right up and down, her gelatinous skin rippling in fiery reds and acid greens, midnight blacks and poisonous yellows.

"Run!" shouts Dr Graveller, as the tentacled monstrosity frees us and instead pins him to the side rail, causing the bag of Gravellerpus remains to fly out of his hand. I manage to catch it as we clamber into the lobby, breathless and soaked.

"We can't leave him out there alone" I yell. "We have to do something, and I think I have a plan."

Tobias' drone has sat unused in his tech-sack for too long. I turn to my scared, wet little brother, "You and Craig are on luring duty, I want you to use the drone to annoy the hell out of that Gravellerpus."

"What are you guys going to do?"

"We're going to save the doctor."

*

With the hose tight in our hands, Felix and I head back out on to the deck. The whole ship is like a rocking horse going back and forth over the attacking waves. Dr Graveller is pinned to the side of the ship underneath a bright orange lifeboat. The Gravellerpus has its tentacles on the lifeboat and around the doctor. I grab Felix and make him follow me to the skybikes.

"NO WAY." He screams above the roar of the ocean. "I'M NOT GETTING ON THE SKYBIKES THE TRACK IS BROKEN."

"IT'S THE ONLY WAY!" I scream back "THINK OF THE PHOTO OPPORTUNITIES." That seems to do the trick. We clamber up onto the stupidly named 'launch pad'.

"DON'T STRAP IN!" I tell Felix

"WHAT?! WHY!" He screams but there's no time to explain...

"FOLLOW ME," I yell, and we peddle off, heading towards the Gravellerpus. The track holding the skybikes is creaking with every lurch of the ship, but we push on. The track up ahead curves sharply down where it has broken and runs straight into the lifeboat.

Right on cue, I see Tobias' drone buzzing around the Gravellerpus like a robotic bee, with the bag of male

Gravellerpus remains tied to its front. The Gravellerpus turns a brilliant scarlet red as it uses all of its tentacles to swipe at the drone. As instructed, Tobias takes the drone higher and higher hovers it by the open lifeboat window and then zooms inside, the Gravellerpus follows. It squeezes its huge body through the tiny window, leaving Dr Graveller behind, winded but alive to crawl back to the lobby doors.

"WHAT NOW!" Felix yells.

"WAIT FOR IT!" I yell back, and sure enough from the lobby I see Craig running out towards the lifeboat. He leaps up at the window and slams it shut, trapping the Gravellerpus within just like Anansi tricking the wasps into the jar.

"NOW!" I yell and I start peddling hard. Felix follows, rushing the skybikes forwards as the ship rocks back and forth.

"FASTER!" I yell and put more speed on. Felix follows suit, until we are moments away from the part of broken track that rests on the lifeboat. We zoom forward and crash our skybikes into the lifeboat, launching it from the ship. The lifeboat falls into the sea with its cargo of monster octopus and disappears into the depths. Our skybikes are about to follow suit. "JUMP!" I yell, grabbing Felix. We leap from the skybikes, the ship's deck rushing up at us.

*

The following day the storm has cleared, and we are sailing in turquoise blue waters as the cruise staff clean the ship. It takes us a while to convince the Captain and our parents that we saved the day. At first they think we're making it up, but then Dr Graveller reveals his research and Felix shows them his photos: incredible photos of a never-seen-before Gravellerpus oozing into the lifeboat, tricked to enter by my amazing little brother and trapped inside by the Captain's own brave son.

"This photo will win me a prize for sure," laughs Felix.

And when Big Ronny wakes from his coma safe and sound he has a tale of his own of being strangled by tentacles which gives him an idea for a new number.

It takes our parents a bit longer to fully forgive us for leaving the safety of the cabin, but by the time we get back home I have a whole new story for Nana to rival anything done by Anansi.

Months later, we see another article about Dr Graveller, who is now keeping his expeditions on land, where it's safer. There's a photo of him in the Congo Basin with Roxy Ravenscroft by his side. As I peer at the photo with my magnifying glass, I spot something crouched in the foliage, something that looks like a gigantic spider! This is going to take some investigating....

A GOOD WEEKEND

THERESA LOLA
ILLUSTRATED BY MOHAMED FADERA

Friday afternoon

We play rock-paper-scissors,
we crack and crease our cheeks, cheese
as we slick our Black hands through the giggling air.
We are at Bellingham Green Park moving
through the grass like paper planes,
flying through the swings as it sings each time we rise.
We play tag, we tag, we tap, we pat, we map.
Our laughter sways and shakes in many tones
forms a sweet melody I want to hear everywhere I go.

Saturday morning

Mum is combing through my Afro from tip to scalp,
then scalp to tip, through strands and sections
held with long clips. I'm sitting still, head stiff,
watching the mirror in front of us mirror us.
My hair springs up, looks like a round ball of fur.
Mum's rubs olive oil on the shining walls of my strands
while she tells me a story.
Her voice breezes through my ears like a fan on a hot day.
The story is about a butterfly teaching a caterpillar about flying.
The story is dipped and mixed with jokes.
Our laughter sways and shakes in many tones,
forms a sweet melody I want to hear everywhere I go.

MOERA.CF
2021

Sunday afternoon

Our living room carpet has turned into a dance floor
thanks to Aunty Celia and Uncle Mark.
Even the clock ticking sounds like a song beat.
Aunty and Uncle's hands swim through the air,
splashes small waves of joy on me.
They say their dance is called an 'electric slide',
that it was popular when they were young.
I show them my moves, the ones we all do at school.
I dish out my dance moves like a cloud pouring rain,
legs flapping, hands clapping, head bopping to the song.
Uncle Mark copies the moves too and it makes us laugh.
Our laughter sways and shakes in many tones
forms a sweet melody I want to hear everywhere I go.

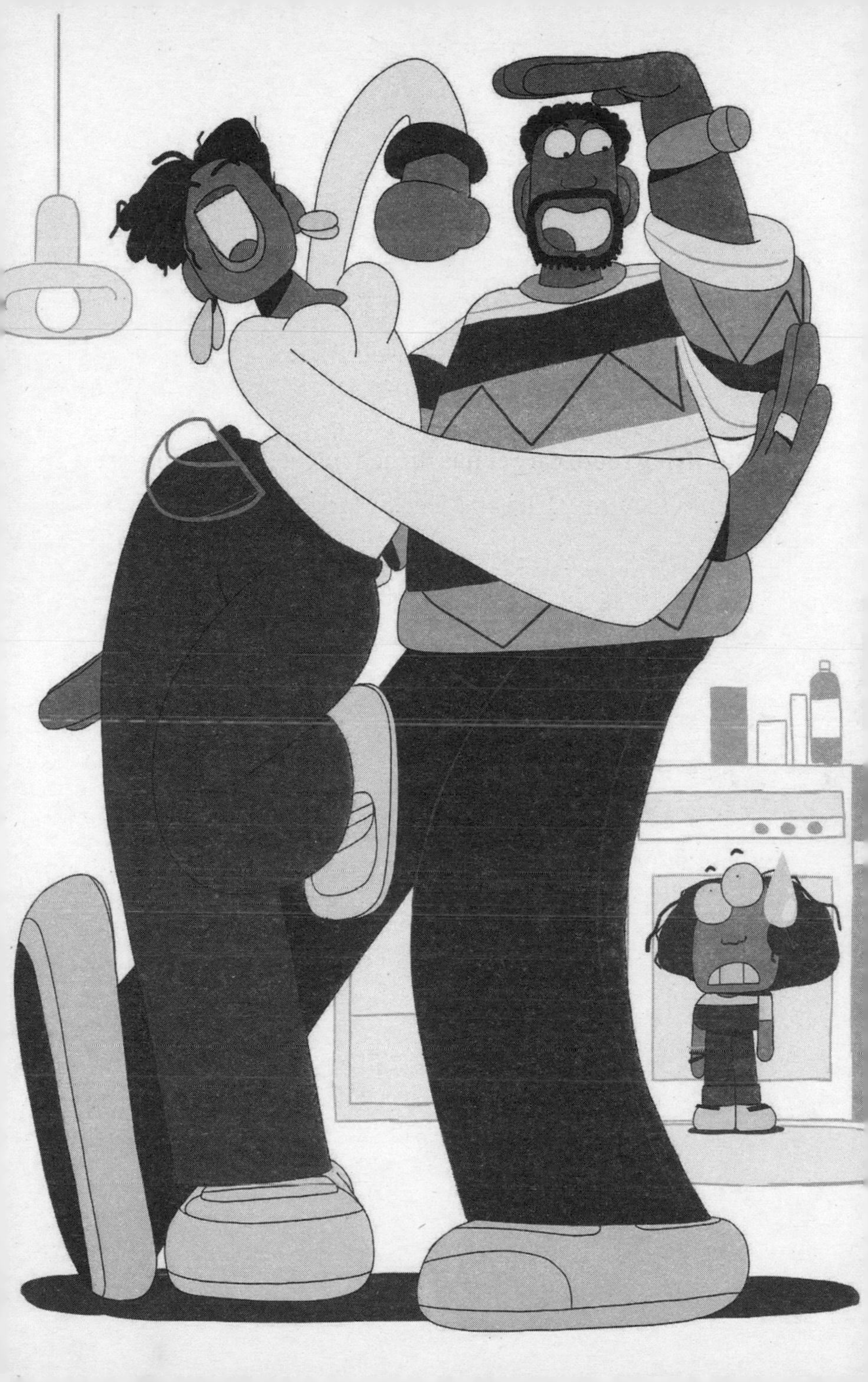

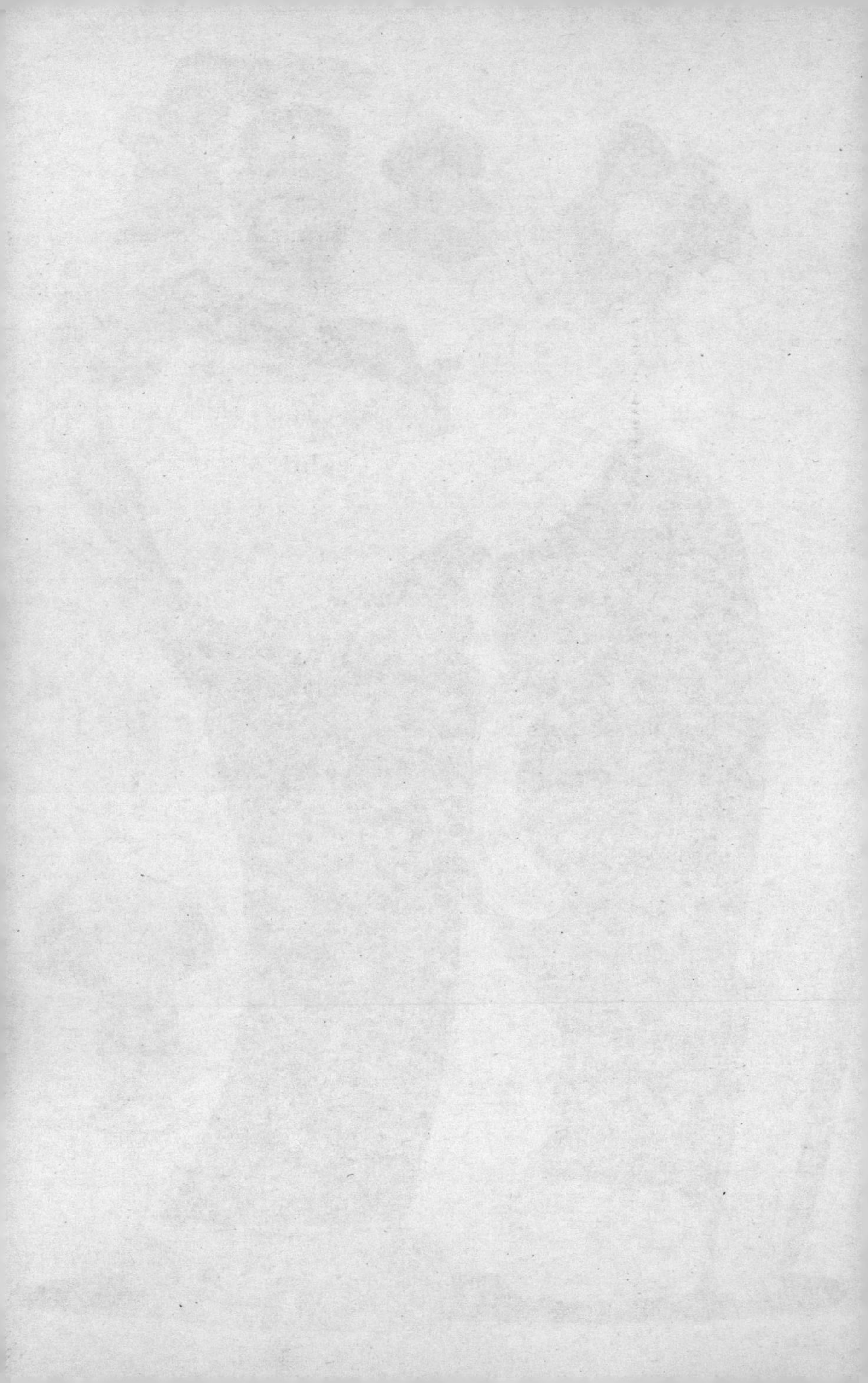

WHERE IS HOME

KEREEN GETTEN
ILLUSTRATED BY LUCY FARFORT

Once a month me and my brother Max go to Dad's for the weekend. Neither of us want to go but Max is the worst. Like sometimes I can't tell if he's genuinely that upset or if he really has lost the plot, because he's a bit of a weird kid anyway.

He'll cry, pretend to have a tummy ache... anything that will keep him home. None of it works. We still have to go.

"Why don't you do something for a change?" Max hisses at me as we climb into Mum's car.

I glare at him."Like what?"

He shrugs his shoulders, still mad that Mum packed his bags in record time after his 'but I'm sick' story failed. “I dunno, pretend to be dead or something.”

I open my phone and start texting my best friend.

“She’ll roll me in the car and say ‘you’ve got to see your dad,’” I mimic Mum’s voice just as she climbs into the car. She spins round to glare at me and Max snorts from the front seat. He likes the front seat. I think it makes him feel important. Like he’s the head of the family or something.

As Mum drives out of our cul-de-sac, I lean forward and nudge my brother.

“Pass the lead,” I whisper. pointing to the car stereo. Mum already has the radio on and is tapping the steering wheel to some old song from five hundred years ago. Max passes me the lead, grinning gleefully because he knows what I’m going to do. I plug the lead into my phone and search for a playlist.

“Can you play my favourite?” he begs. I skim through my list and press play before Mum knows what is happening. Music blasts through the car and she jumps, sending Max into a fit of giggles.

“April!” She shouts over the music. She reaches for the volume but Max stops her.

“Mum,” he begs, “we can’t go to Dad’s and listen to your old music, that’s not fair.”

She screws her eyes at him, but she can never say no to a

good digging at Dad. It's like her energy drink or something and Max knows that. It's how he gets what he wants.

"Fine," she groans, "just turn it down, and it's not old music thank you very much." She glares at me in the rear-view mirror. "You lot—"

"—don't appreciate good music," me and Max finish off for her.

My dad Renald lives in a posh block of flats, right across from a park with a lake and swans and stuff. There's a security man inside the foyer, who sits behind a high desk so you can only see his eyes. He watches everyone that comes in to see if he knows you, and, if he doesn't, he tries to race you to the lift to kick you out. Max thinks this is hilarious and walks really fast pretending he can't hear him.

This time though he stops us at the entrance. "Mr Herman isn't back from work yet," he says. "He left a message saying he's running late."

Mum mumbles something under her breath about Dad having all our numbers but not using one of them to let us know. We walk into the foyer and sit on these red sofas that are shaped like massive lips.

Max starts to moan again. It's like his brain switches between remembering he doesn't want to be here and all the other random stuff boys think about.

"I knew we shouldn't have come," he moans folding his arms against his chest. "I could be playing online with Dion."

Mum tells him not to start, but it's like he hears 'carry on, but be louder this time.'

Mum's phone rings and she passes it to me. "It's your dad," she says, because she never talks to him unless it's absolutely necessary and that's annoying. Like, they're both grownups so why can't they sort it out between them? I take the phone reluctantly.

"April?" I can hear the noise of his car. "I'm sorry, I was caught up with work and—"

"It's okay," I mumble. Max kicks me. No it's not, he mouths. I stand up and walk away from him.

"I'll be there in a few minutes. I'm just around the corner."

He's not. He definitely just left his office.

"Okay."

"Tell him I can't wait much longer," Mum shouts over at me. I try to block her out by covering my left ear.

"What did your mum say?"

"Nothing."

"Okay, I'll be there before you've even hung up, bye."

I hang up. Mum and Max are both frowning at me so I

sit away from them both. Everyone seems to think I'm their spokesperson and that annoys me because I'm not.

Dad arrives forty minutes later. That's about the same time it takes to drive from his office to his flat. He runs in apologising, and ignores Mum while calling me and Max to follow him to the lift. He and Mum barely talk anymore. It's like they're strangers the way they carry on. Like they were never married for ten years. Adults are weird like that. They spend hundreds of years together then have one argument and never speak again... and they call us the kids.

Mum shakes her head in disgust at Dad and hugs us both. "Be good," she says, and watches us leave.

When we get in the lift, Dad's phone starts ringing and he answers it while trying to hold on to his briefcase and a ton of papers. But as soon as the lift starts to move, he loses the call and I feel a little smug about that.

"Hello? Hello?" He shouts down the phone, "this happens every time."

The doors open on the 12th floor and we follow him out, as he tries to call back the person he was talking to. I hold out my hand for the key, and he fumbles in his pocket and hands it to me as his call connects.

"John...yeah...I lost you in the lift...so did we get it?"

I unlock the door of his flat and enter the long narrow hallway with Max close behind. We walk to the end of the hall, which opens up into a living room and a kitchen with windows overlooking the city. I throw my bag on the floor and slump into the sofa, Max grabs the games console to turn it on.

Dad enters the living room and snaps his fingers at us while still on the call. He gestures for the console, and then to me for my phone. "Yes...I agree...that's the only way forward...alright John let's catch up Monday."

He ends the call and looks at us both with raised eyebrows, "You know the rules when you're over here. Phones and console for an hour on Saturday only. This isn't your mum's house where you stare at machines all day." There's that dig at Mum, and it's only taken him two minutes and thirty-three seconds.

"But what else am I supposed to do?" Max moans, not willing to hand over the only thing that gets him through the weekend.

"The world is full of possibilities, Max. Hand it over."

Max begrudgingly hands him the console.

"Right," he says, "I'll be in my office, try and keep the noise down please." He takes my phone, the console, his other important stuff and heads down the hall to his bedroom that doubles as his office. The door closes, and then it's silent.

Max storms off to his room and slams the door, and I slump back into the sofa wondering how I'm going to get through another weekend.

Later that evening, a pizza arrives for me and Max. Dad left us twenty pounds to order something for dinner. I manage to coax Max out of his room when I tell him I got his favourite pizza, and we both sit on stools behind the breakfast bar.

The flat is quiet and it's nothing like home where Mum would be singing while cooking dinner.

"Let's get our stuff back from Dad," I tell Max because I know he loves playing games.

"But he said we can't have our stuff," he says, stating the obvious.

I roll my eyes. "I never said we were going to ask for it, Max." When he's still blank faced, I spell it out, "I'll distract him and you get the stuff."

His eyes light up. "Like my favourite PS4 game?"

I frown. "What? No, nothing like that." He follows me down the hall. "Just do what you do at Mum's when she hides your presents."

Max could never wait until Christmas Day for his presents and would spend hours searching for Mum's hiding place.

We reach Dad's door and he's on the phone. I turn to Max, who is so excited I'm scared he'll give us away. "Be calm." I instruct him firmly. He nods excitedly, "I will."

I knock on the door and open it. Dad is still on the phone, so I nudge Max to sneak over to the drawers where we know our things are kept. I stand with my back against the wall, in Dad's view so he can only see me, while Max creeps across the room.

Finally, Dad ends the call and looks up. "What is it, April?" he says, shortly.

"We left some pizza for you," I say, walking around the back of his chair to block Max. "Do you want me to bring you a slice?"

Dad shakes his head. "No, in fact, I was going to ask Mary from across the way to keep an eye on you while I nip out for a few drinks, is that okay?"

The drawer slams and Max storms towards the door. I think he's putting on a show to throw Dad off the scent, so I allow him his moment because Max does like his moment.

"Max? What's the matter? And why were you in my drawer?"

Max spins round and he's crying, real tears. This is either his best performance yet or he really is upset.

"I don't understand why we're here." He cries through

tears. "You take all our stuff away and then you go out with your friends."

"I have to work Max," Dad says irritably, "it's how I can afford this flat and your console." Max wipes his snotty face with the back of his hands. "But what do you need us here for?"

There is a pause and I want to look at Dad because even I know Max has crossed the line, but all I can see is the back of Dad's head.

"Because I want to see you," Dad says, a little less angry this time.

"Doesn't feel like it," Max says, "when people want to see you, they do things with you, not lock you in a flat and then work all the time."

Dad pushes his chair back, "Max—"

"I don't want to be here," Max shouts. "I want to call Mum and get her to pick me up. I hate it here." He opens the door and runs out. The door slams behind him and I don't even know if he got the stuff.

Dad turns his chair to face me and his forehead is wrinkled. "Is that how you feel too?" he asks. I know what he wants me to say, that Max is being dramatic and I don't agree with him, and normally I would but this time I agree with Max, he just chose a strange time to say it.

I move away as if the distance will make it easier to answer his question, but even that isn't enough for me to tell the truth, because no matter how mad I am with Dad; I still find it hard to tell him how I feel. Maybe I'm afraid that telling him the truth will make him run further away from us. So instead, I shrug half-heartedly and follow Max out the door and it is only when I am in the hall that I feel my heart thundering against my chest.

I open Max's door and peer in. "Did you get it?"

He throws a pillow at me. "Go away."

I catch the pillow and walk over to his bed. I stand over him, knowing all he wants is Mum because she would give him a hug and a kiss and tell him he was right and Dad was wrong. I lay on the bed next to him and wrap my arms around him even though his arms are folded tightly against his chest.

My brother Max was never one to hide his feelings. We're completely different like that. He has at least twenty outbursts a day, but then he will be over it in ten minutes. I was more like Mum, holding things in, pretending everything is okay just to keep the peace. There didn't seem any point in both of us losing it. One of us had to keep it together.

But sometimes, like now, I wish I was more like Max, because at least he had the courage to say what was on his mind.

It is still dark when I am woken suddenly. "April, it's me, Dad."

The bedside lamp is switched on and he is looking down at me. "Get dressed," he says trying to sound cheerful, "we're going on an adventure."

A bleary-eyed Max rolls over. "What's going on?" he mumbles. Dad throws a pair of jeans and jumper on the bed before turning to Max.

"We're going on an adventure," he repeats, "so get dressed."

My dad didn't do adventures. Not the kind of adventures normal people do. He never climbed Mount Everest or swam with sharks. Dad's biggest claim to adventure was changing his university two years into his course. He tells that story all the time, as though he's telling you he stopped a robbery. So, when he dragged us out of bed at 4am on Saturday morning saying we were going on an adventure, I was sceptical.

Things continued to get strange when we climbed into the car. It was still dark outside and Dad's humming a song I don't know but it annoys me because I don't know why he's so cheerful.

"Right, who's ready for an adventure?" He's said the word adventure fifteen times now. He's using it as though it's some sort of magic word that will change everything and make us like him again.

"Can I get my phone on this adventure?" I ask.

He shakes his head wagging his finger at me. "Nice try though peanut, nice try."

Peanut was his nickname for me because he said I looked like one when I was born. It used to be funny when he lived with us. When he liked us enough to stay, but now it feels like an insult. I slump into the back seat and pull the blanket over me.

When I wake, the car is stationary and Max and Dad are nowhere to be seen. I throw the covers off and climb out of the car rubbing sleep from my eyes. We are in a car park by some railings and I spot the sea in the horizon. I walk over to the railings and see Max and Dad sitting on an embankment leading down to a brown, pebbled beach.

It's quiet, except for a few seagulls ,and Max is chattering non-stop about how he's always wanted to be at the seaside while chomping down on a sandwich.

"I don't even mind that it's a bit cold," he says with his mouth full, "it's still better than being at home." Dad chuckles and wipes a stray crumb off his cheek. I step over the railings and head down the embankment to where they are.

"Oh, she's awake," Dad says catching me when I slip. I sit down next to him and he hands me a breakfast sandwich.

"Aww," Max moans. "You said I could have her sandwich."

"If she didn't wake up soon, I said," Dad replies nudging Max. He turns to me. "It's no-good cold." I take a bite of the sandwich and try to ignore the fact that he was going to give my sandwich to Max and let me starve.

I've noticed Max has changed his tune from last night. Now he's acting like him and Dad are best friends. That boy has no loyalty.

Now they're both laughing at a seagull trying to steal Max's food. I can't bear it any longer.

"You having a good time Max?" I say through clenched teeth. He frowns, leaning forward to look at me. When he sees my face, his smile disappears. He leans back so I can't see him. "I was only talking about the birds," he mumbles.

"And the sea, and the sandwich," I retort, "what were you talking about last night? You forgotten?" Max falls silent.

If he's going to be mad at Dad, I wish he would stick to that and not keep changing every five minutes. Dad looks at me for some time before speaking. "Is there something you want to say April?"

"No."

"Because now is the time."

Why is now the time? Why wasn't it the time last night, or last week, or when he walked out on us? What's so special about now?

Dad stands. "Right, let's take a walk down the promenade, there's lots to do down there."

Max jumps to his feet and climbs the hill quickly after Dad, as though he's trying to get away from me. He and Dad walk ahead along a small path that snakes along the bridge of the embankment. A few people with dogs walk by, and in the distance, you can see the town. Max jumps up and down, begging Dad to let him go on the Ferris wheel. They're laughing as though last night never happened. As

if he hasn't been the worst dad in the world who left us and thought nothing of it. Max has a short memory and its annoying me that he switches so quickly. What happens when this beach day is over and we go back to boring life in the city? When Dad goes back to work and ignores us again? Who is he going to run to then?

I try to keep up with Dad and Max but they disappear between bodies and I'm forced to run to catch up with them. The path is no longer quiet. It's filled with laughter and music coming from the Ferris wheel. I can see Max tugging at Dad and pointing to the wheel.

They haven't looked round once to see if I'm still here.

It makes me wonder if this trip was for me at all. Maybe it was for Max and I was forced along by default.

Before Max came along, Dad and I were close. We did everything together. Even when Max came along, with all his needy mood swings, Dad always put aside time for me and him. It was always Max and Mum, me and Dad. Maybe that's why Max made such a big deal about seeing Dad on the weekends, he knew he wouldn't get the same attention Mum gave him.

Now, it's as if they were always best friends. Now, I'm the third wheel and all it took was a trip to the seaside and a breakfast sandwich.

I suddenly bump into someone and look up. It's Dad.

"Keep up April," he says, "we'll lose you otherwise, and we don't want that do we, Max?"

Max snorts. "I might want to lose her." He says, and suddenly I feel an overwhelming sense of betrayal from my brother. Didn't I try to help him out last night? Wasn't I the one who came up with the genius plan to get the phones, except he ruined it? Am I not the one who is constantly trying to cheer him up when he's upset about something or other to do with Dad? Now he wants me to disappear?

"Why don't you disappear Max?" I snap. "Then I don't have to listen to you moaning every day about how much you hate Dad."

People push past us and the music is still playing, but it might as well have been silent for the heavy air that surrounds us. Max pouts, then grimaces. His fists tighten and I think he's going to lob one on me but instead he screams, "I hate you," and runs off into the crowd.

Deep down, I know I only said it to ruin whatever fun he was having with Dad. It worked.

Dad looks at me gravely, then runs after Max calling his name because of course he goes after Max, the favourite child.

I stand in the middle of the crowd, wondering if he would run after me in the same way.

I find a seat on the edge of the path, between a hotdog stand and a balloon machine. It's one of those old wooden chairs you see old people sitting on, eating homemade sandwiches.

Seconds later, Dad reappears looking frantic.

"April," he cries out of breath, "have you seen your brother? I can't find him."

My breath catches in my throat. "But he was just there," I point down the path.

"Yes," he says impatiently, "but I can't find him." He looks up and down the path and I've never seen Dad look so worried.

"Maybe he's gone to the fair or something," he starts to walk again, "and stay with me this time April, I can't lose both of you."

I follow behind him as he squeezes through crowds, around people, occasionally looking behind him to make sure I am still there. We search the stalls, and scan the brown pebbled beach. The more time we spend looking for my brother, the faster my father walks, until it's almost impossible to keep up with him.

"Dad," I shout after him, "slow down."

He stops, "April, I'm trying to find your brother, keep up."

"I can't keep up; you're going too fast."

"Then walk faster," he snaps. I stop suddenly in the middle of the promenade.

"I didn't even want to come here; Max didn't want to come here. You forced us and now you've lost him."

I can't believe I said that. My heart pounds inside my chest.

He storms back towards me wagging his finger at me. "You might not want to be here, April, but your brother did."

"He didn't." I shout. "He didn't even want to see you. He begged Mum to not send him. He hates it with you."

He stares at me, the agitation on his face mixed with something else, something I haven't seen before. I keep going.

"You think we want to come to your flat just to sit by ourselves and order pizza for dinner? We can do that at Mum's. At least she'll sit with us. At least Mum tries."

"We don't have time for this," he says through clenched teeth, glancing at the curious eyes around us. I shrug, suddenly feeling brave amongst all these people. It's as if once I started talking, I couldn't stop. "There's never a good time, because you never listen to us. You never ask us anything."

Dad takes a deep breath and pauses. He closes his eyes. When he opens them, he looks at me differently. "I hear you April," he says slowly as if choosing his words carefully. "But can we find your brother first?"

Maybe it's the security of the crowds. Maybe it's the frustration boiling to the top. Or maybe I just couldn't keep these feeling hidden any longer.

"I want to go home."

"We will." His voice is steady. "Just as soon as we find your brother."

"Not your home. My home. I want Mum to pick me up."

A flicker of hurt shades his eyes so clearly. "You want to go back to your mother's?" There is an edge in his voice. "Okay, but first, let's find your brother."

He takes my hand tightly, leading me through the crowd, not trusting me to follow behind. Part of me feels betrayed that I am not more triumphant at my achievement. Part of me feels upset he didn't fight harder.

"There he is." He lets go of my hand as we enter the small amusement park on the pier. Max is standing in the queue for the Ferris wheel. Dad pushes through the line, apologising to everyone and drags Max out of the line.

Max is not happy. "I've lost my place now."

Dad goes into a long tirade of the usual, 'don't ever run off like that, anyone could have taken you, you had me worried sick,' and the popular, 'you can't get away with this like you can with your mother.'

I would say he's the only one who says that but he's not, Mum says the same thing. They use each other's name to prove they are the better parent. Like they are each the ones that got parenting right.

He continues lecturing Max as we leave the pier, him holding on to Max and me trailing behind.

He finds a café just off the promenade. The waitress leads us over to a table by the window and we sit down, Max next to Dad, and me across from them both.

"I don't understand why I can't go on the Ferris wheel," Max moans burying his face in his hands.

"Stop going on about the stupid Ferris wheel." Me and Dad say at the same time. We lock eyes and he smiles briefly before his eyes cloud over as though he remembers something.

Max pouts at me."You're supposed to be on my side."

I roll my eyes. "Stop being such a baby Max."

"I'm not being a baby. Don't call me that."

I lean forward on the table lowering my head to match his. "You're being a baby. You were a baby when you ran off because you couldn't wait five minutes for us to go to the stupid fair, and you're a baby for not thinking about how worried Dad was. All you think about is yourself. Grow up."

I lean back on my chair and fold my arms against my chest staring out the window. The table falls silent until the waitress interrupts us to ask what we want. Dad orders the same for all of us, fish and chips and three orange juices. The waitress leaves and Dad says, "You know you don't have to be his parent April. That's not your job."

I feel my fingers clench, and my mouth tightens. "Whose job is it then?" I ask, chancing a look at him. He opens his mouth to answer, then closes it leaning back in his chair.

The thing is, Max has always seemed like my responsibility. I was the only one who understood his mood swings, his tears, and his craziness. Mum treated him like a baby, and Dad just snapped at him. I glance over at Max; it was no wonder he was so confused sometimes.

The food arrives and Max is the only one who tucks in, because Max has already forgotten that he was upset.

I play around with my food, not really having an appetite. Dad moves something across the table and it's my phone. I look up and he smiles weakly, like when adults try and fake their emotions.

"To call your mum," he says, "you can go in the doorway where it's quieter but no further." I take the phone hesitantly. This feels like a trick. I glance over at him but he is talking to Max about what he wants to do next.

"Ferris wheel!" Max says immediately, his mouth full of chips. I push my chair back and walk out of the restaurant and into the small entrance between the first door and the second. I glance through the glass doors at Dad and Max, suddenly feeling guilty. I look down at the phone in my hand, then take a breath and dial the number. Mum picks up almost immediately because Mum thinks something bad has happened every time we call.

"April? What's happened?"

I lean against the wall of the café. "Nothing,"

"Is your brother okay?"

I sigh staring at the ceiling. "Yes."

She sighs the same way I do and it sounds as though she sits down. "What's the matter then? Where are you?"

"At the seaside."

She gets upset again. “The what? What are you doing at the seaside? Has your dad handed you over to that babysitter again? What’s the matter with him? Why can’t he do his job?” She goes off on a rant. The same rant I hear from both them except the name changes and that’s when I realise, it’s not just Dad, it’s both of them.

“Do you want to come home?” Mum says worriedly.

“Where is that?” I say, quietly kicking my shoe against the tiled floor and suddenly I can feel the tears brimming.

“What do you mean, where is that? It’s here with me,” she says. I kick the tiles harder, hoping it will stop me from crying.

“April? Are you still there?” she asks down the phone. I bite my lip hard but the tears come anyway.

“It doesn’t feel like it,” and now I’m crying through the words, “nowhere feels like home anymore.”

I wipe the tears away furiously but they return faster, and now I can barely get the words out, I’m crying so hard.

“Oh April,” she says down the phone. She falls silent until my crying subsides.

“April, your home is with me and your father,” she says, with a strain of regret in her voice. “Your home is wherever you feel the safest, and we want you to feel safe and loved with both of us. So, you’re right. Home is not just with me. Home is with your father too." When I don't answer she says, "you go back to whatever you're doing, and we'll talk later."

When I return to the table, Dad's phone rings and he leaves the table. "Hello?" he says surprised, and I know Mum has called him.

When he returns to the table, he seems different. "So, can we go to the Ferris wheel now?" Max asks excitedly. Dad nods but he seems preoccupied and he keeps glancing over at me.

He leans his elbows on the table, "You know, when I came from Jamaica to England without my parents it was really scary," he says.

Max stops mid eating to ask; "You came to England without your parents?"

Dad nods. "I was ten years old, and my mum sent me to England to live with my aunt so I could have a better life. I remember how scared I was to be without her, but how determined I was to make her proud."

I chance a glance at him and he's staring at the food, playing with his fork the same way I am.

"I didn't know you could get on a plane at ten." Max says. "That's so cool."

Dad chuckles. "Yeah, it was cool Max. It was my first

time on an aeroplane too." He sighs. "Anyway, my point is, I became obsessed with being successful so my mum would be proud. So obsessed, I forgot what it was like to have parents around. I forgot what it was like to give my kids the one thing I missed the most from my mum."

I stare hard at the plate, determined not to give him what he wants, a reaction. I know what he's doing telling these sob stories, trying to get on our good side again.

"Anyway, I'm sorry," he says, "I'm sorry for not remembering what it's like to be present." I feel him looking directly at me but I don't give him any eye contact, mostly because I don't want him to see my bloodshot eyes.

Max lays a hand on Dad's. "I forgive you… if you let me go on the Ferris wheel."

Max gets to go on the Ferris wheel twice, even though I don't think he deserved it even once.

"Let's do something April wants to do now," Dad says, nudging me. "What do you want to do, April?"

"She doesn't do anything but text on her phone," Max grumbles.

"What about the game we used to play at the lake?" Dad suggests, ignoring Max. Every Saturday afternoon we would all go to the park. Mum would take Max to the swings and Dad would take me to the lake to skim stones across the water. He nudges me again with a glint in his eye.

On the pebbled beach Dad teaches Max how to skim rocks into the sea. They laugh and cheer when they get it right and I sit on my jacket watching from a distance.

Max makes his way over to me in his hunched over way; he does it as though life is exhausting. "Come on!" he says. "You can't be moody forever."

I tell him to sit down beside me and he does with his usual groan.

"What?" He moans, not even looking at me. I nudge him until he does. "I spoke to Mum."

He shrugs. "Yeah, so?"

"So, she's not mad at Dad anymore. She wants us to like it at Dads'. She wants us to call it home."

He thinks about this for a second, then his head falls to his chest. "She said that?"

A lump forms in my throat as I realise Max has been doing the same thing I have. Protecting Mum. Forcing ourselves to hate it at Dad's so she wouldn't feel betrayed, because we owed her that right? She was the one who stayed after all.

He gets up suddenly with a new lease of energy. "So you coming to play or what?"

I follow him down to where Dad is waiting patiently. He hands me a stone and I bend my knees, twist my arm, and flick the stone low. It spins and skims the waves, one, two, three times. I jump in the air eyes wide with shock that I had done it first time.

"How did you do that?" Max pouts.

Dad high fives me, April First Time I smile from ear to ear, my heart feeling something I have not felt in a long while.

"Do it again," Max says, "or it's beginners' luck."

I walk to the edge of the beach, turn sideways, squint into the horizon and flick another stone. It skims the waves, one, two, three, four times. I turn to them arms in the air, triumphant a second time.

"Oh! She did it a second time," Dad shouts, hitting my outstretched hand, "this can be no coincidence, this can only be sheer talent."

Max looks at the stones in his hands, then at me frowning. "First one to ten wins," Max says "and then we go home and maybe play on the console?" He looks to Dad hesitantly, almost nervously.

Dad's eyes beam and his smile is wide. "We can definitely play a few games when we get home," he says. I think he wants to make sure Max hadn't said home by mistake.

Max grins at me and we get ready for another game. But this feels more than a game of stones. This feels like the start of something new.

YOU'RE THE BOSS.

E.L. NORRY
ILLUSTRATED BY CHANTÉ TIMOTHY

Autumn term and the first day at your new school. You've just gotten over a bad virus, so you missed a few days, but hopefully, that won't be a problem. This week is induction for the whole of Year Seven. Just Year Seven. The older pupils don't start until next week, which is a relief.

Walking through the tall imposing school gates, you're self-conscious. You squirm - this uniform is so stiff! You didn't have a jacket at your old school. A blazer. You feel weird, like you stand out. You liked being the oldest at your primary school but now it feels like you're starting all over again. There are butterflies in your stomach.

You didn't even want to move to this tiny town. It's so

different! The school classes only have fifteen children each. You'll get more 'attention', but you don't want more attention. You like blending into the background, thanks very much. You miss the noise of the big city, and your mates too. You really miss your mates.

Across the playground, boys and girls line up. All you can see is a sea of black and navy. No bright colours anywhere. That's because your school bag has to be black or navy, and so does your coat. Your pencil case has to be clear plastic and exactly 20cm. This place doesn't seem keen on individuality or trust, from what you can tell so far.

A teacher, dressed all in black, stands at the front of a line. She's holding up a sign that says CLASS X. You check the slip of paper with your registration details on that your clutching – X. You join the queue.

"Class X," the teacher says, "follow me. You know the drill by now: leave your phones and devices in the reception tray. You may collect at the end of the day. Thank you."

Students file through the double doors into school. Each of them drops their mobile phone into a large plastic tray on the reception desk as they pass.

What? No phones?

Leaning forward, you whisper to the boy in front of you. "What's with the phone thing?"

He turns to stare at you. "Hi. Oh, you're new," he says, tilting his head to one side. "You hand over your phone - anything electronic - when you step through the doors," he says, smiling.

"And if I don't?" you joke.

A frown appears. "You must," he replies. "You have to follow the rules."

"Seems a bit strict?"

He blinks rapidly. "It's great here. It's our gaming session this morning."

"Computer Studies?"

He grins. "No. Just wait 'til we get to class. You'll see."

2.

You follow Class X down long white corridors. On the walls are colourful images of different countries. Your old school was full of photos of student and class achievements, but here there are just images of vast landscapes: mountains and volcanos; fields and oceans.

The snaking line heads into a classroom. Everyone glides smoothly into their seats. You can't believe what they're sitting in front of - the classroom looks like a dream! Three rows of five seats, each row with a Playstation, X-Box or PC on the desk.

The teacher beckons you to the front.

"I'm Miss Perkulea. Welcome! We've been looking forward to having you start with us, here at Quiverly High." As she smiles, her lips stick to her top teeth.

"Tell us about yourself," she says. "We'd like to get to know you, wouldn't we, class X?"

"Yes Miss Perkulea," fourteen smiling faces chant back.

Weird.

Opening your mouth, you wince as only a squeak comes out. Remember what your best mate Deepak texted this morning: Show them who's the boss, right?! It'll be okay. Call me at lunchtime.

You clear your throat. "Hi," you raise your hand and give a little wave. "I'm Ash. I like..." You rack your brain for things you enjoy that no-one can be judgy about. "I like riding my bike, playing computer games and drawing."

"Good job!" Miss Perkulea claps her hands together delighted, as if this is the most exciting thing she's ever heard. "We're glad to have you join us, Ash. Sorry you missed the rest of the week, but you'll settle in. We've got Gaming this morning, then after lunch it's our final inoculations before the field trip."

You're relieved the attention is off you for now.

"Take a seat in the middle row, next to Meera and Billie. You'll soon fit right in."

You sit down - right in front of a Playstation 5 complete with VR headset. Amazing! You can't believe you'll get to play video games in school. You guess they'll be educational in some way, but it's still pretty cool.

What kind of school is this?

Miss Perkulea says, "You might have heard from friends in Classes Y and Z that for the first 20-minute gaming session, we all play the same game: Apix Destiny Operation." She smiles and walks around the classroom switching on the machines.

"After your scores have come in, we'll put you on one of the other three games, by the appropriate stream. It'll tell us which level you're at and what you need to focus on. Once your games have loaded, you may begin!"

The game loads.

"Have you just moved here?" Meera murmurs, sweeping her long, black hair out of her eyes, once Miss Perkulea has gone to the back of the class.

"Yeah," you reply. "It's pretty different to where I used to live. Really... quiet."

Meera snorts. "Everyone thinks nothing happens in a town like this because it's small but that's not true."

You narrow your eyes. "What do you mean?"

"Things aren't always what they seem. You can't judge by appearances." Meera glances around furtively. "So, you haven't had your—"

3.

Suddenly, a kid bursts in, looking frantic. His white shirt is untucked and muddy, and his tie flaps loose. His hair is practically standing on end. His eyes are wide, and he looks wildly around before running over to the windows. He starts banging on them.

Another teacher comes in and rushes over to him.

"You won't get me!" the boy screams, backing into a corner. He picks up a chair and holds it out as if trying to tame a lion.

"Now, now," the teacher says calmly, holding out his arms. "Drop that chair before someone gets hurt." His voice is low and steady, but the kid looks deranged, flinging his head from side to side, desperate.

He drops the chair, and his eyes light up as he sees you. "You!" He points at you. "You're new too! Don't let them fool you."

What's he talking about?

Before he heads your way, the teacher grabs him under the arms and drags him across the room. The boy's black shoes scrape along the floor, the rubber squeaking, leaving black streaks. Just before the door slams shut, the boy locks eyes with you, mouthing, 'Get out!' before being hauled into the corridor.

You're totally shocked. Teachers can't do that to students! Can they? He looked terrified.

"Class X!" Miss Perkulea clears her throat. "What a disruption. It won't happen again. Now, where were we?"

No one else seems bothered by what just happened but your heart is beating fast. What was that all about? And why did the boy want to speak to you?

Miss Perkulea comes around to your side of the desk. "I'm sorry, Ash," she says. "Really, it's nothing to worry about. The boy is from Z class and has been struggling to... adjust this week. Went off the rails after his gaming lesson. He has behaviour problems, emotional difficulties. But it's all taken care of now."

Miss Perkulea goes to sit behind her desk. Her eyes are half-closed; she almost looks like she's meditating.

"Focus, everyone. In the gaming zone please!"

You glance around. Everyone is deep into their games. Meera and Billie concentrate, jabbing at their joysticks so fast that their brown fingers are a blur.

You've never been in a classroom this silent. It feels...

strange. Unnatural somehow. You expected 'big school' to be different, but not quite like this. You've heard that if you don't behave, some secondary schools can give out detentions, isolations, and even suspensions. Was this school that strict? Is that why everyone was so well behaved?

That boy didn't look naughty to you. He just looked scared. The question is who, or what, is he scared of?

START THE ADVENTURE

CHOICE: You're the boss. Which do you choose?

A: Ask a classmate about the boy who just burst in (stay on this page)

B: Keep quiet and investigate later (go to page 136)

A: Ask a classmate about the student who just burst in

You lean across your desk and tap Meera on the shoulder.

"What's up with Freak-Out Boy?" you whisper.

Meera glances around the classroom, making sure Miss Perkulea is still in her half-meditative state. "Before he burst in, I was going to ask – have you had your first jab yet?" She pushes up the glasses on her nose.

You frown, confused. "My what?"

"That kid who freaked out?" Meera lowers her voice. "He's not the only kid to act like that. I've seen two this week, both from the other classes and I think it's to do with--"

"Excuse me?!" Miss Perkulea's voice rings out sharply across the classroom, and before you can blink, she's directly in front of you. "Stop this talking at once!"

Her eyes are bright blue and piercing. Her friendliness from before has melted away and she towers over you, staring intensely.

"How dare you be so rude! We will not tolerate you disrupting other students. I suggest you go and visit the Headmaster's office immediately."

CHOICE: You're the boss! Which do you choose?

A: Go straight to the Headmaster's office (stay on this page)

B: Instead of going to the Headmaster's office, you sneak off to reception to ask for your phone (go to page 129)

A: Go straight to the Headmaster's office

You can't believe it's your first day and you're in trouble already! Your parents will be so disappointed. You hoped this school would be a fresh start.

Walking slowly down the corridor, you follow the signs for

the Headmaster's office. Strangely, for a school, the place is eerily quiet. What did Meera mean, about jabs, and the other kids who'd been acting weirdly?

When you reach the end of the corridor, the door marked 'Headmaster's Office' is open an inch or two. There's no desk, or a Headmaster. The room is small and stuffy, with no windows and a strong smell of antiseptic. A blue curtain divides the room. It reminds you of the sick bay at your old school. Have you got the wrong room?

Just as you're about to walk out, a man emerges from behind the curtain.

"I'm Mr Lotcorn." Spindly fingers brush away a lank fringe hanging in his eyes. "You've been sent here for..." he narrows his eyes. "Disturbing the classroom, I understand."

That's putting it a bit strongly, you think.

He hands you a large pair of headphones. "Put these on, please." He points to a chair in front of the curtain. "Sit there and listen to these soothing sounds. They'll help you relax and calm down."

What? You don't need to calm down. There's nothing wrong with you! You just asked a question and then got sent here!

Just how strict is this school?

But you know you'll have to do as you're told, so you sit down and put on the headphones.

In a short while, over the sound of crashing sea waves, you hear a ringtone. Mr Lotcorn emerges and removes his mobile phone from his jacket on the door. After listening for a bit, he puts the phone back in his jacket pocket. He glances at you briefly, then leaves the room in a hurry.

In your ears, the noise of the sea raises to an annoying dolphin squeak, so you take them off. You lean forward in your chair and peep behind the curtain. There you glimpse the same boy who came into your lesson earlier. The one who got dragged off!

You pull back the curtain fully now. The boy sits on a bench, rocking gently back and forth, staring at the floor. Now, he looks calm, with his uniform immaculate and his hair combed, but it's definitely the same boy.

"Hey," you say. "You alright?"

The boys stares at the ground, dazed.

"Everything okay?" You go over and gently shake his shoulder.

"Where am I?" he asks, shaking his head. His voice is expressionless. His eyes are glassy and it's as if he's looking... through you. You shiver.

Suddenly you hear raised voices and footsteps outside.

You quickly close the curtain and sit back down. Putting the headphones on, now all you can hear is a distorted hiss.

Mr Lotcorn comes in, glances at you briefly, and disappears behind the curtain. You pull the headphones down round your neck and strain to hear what he's saying but you can't make out any words.

Soon Mr Lotcorn emerges with the boy and leads him to the door. The boy glances over his shoulder at you. His eyes are fearful and pleading and he gives a tiny nod towards the curtain where Mr Lotcorn has left his jacket.

CHOICE: You're the boss! Which do you choose?

A: You go through Mr Lotcorn's jacket pockets (stay on this page)

B: You follow Mr Lotcorn and the boy, at a distance (go to page 127)

A: You go through Mr Lotcorn's jacket pockets

You're relieved to find Mr Lotcorn's phone in his jacket pocket. You take it out and are glad to see that it's still unlocked. Your fingers tremble as you search for his voicemail. You select the latest message and play it.

"Assimilation is almost complete." A lisping voice rasps, sounding like several voices overlapping. "Bring all subjects into the assembly hall for 'Relaxation Time'. Once they're on the mats, we'll release the sleeping formula. After fifteen minutes, their neurons will be permanently altered."

What's happening? 'Assimilation' doesn't sound good! 'Subjects' – that must mean you and the other pupils!

You have to do something, quickly! How can you stop the other pupils from being sent to the assembly hall?

You run down the corridor, looking all around you, trying to think of a solution.

You spy a fire alarm on the wall. If you broke it, that could buy some time. With the tiny hammer, you break the glass and press the alarm.

The noise which rings out is deafening. Doors all along the corridor fly open and the year sevens rush out. The kids all head towards the main exit, while the teachers swarm together behind them, looking more and more agitated and holding their ears. The high-pitched ringing seems to be making them very distressed. This is the first time you've noticed any strong reaction from them at all.

Then, the weirdest thing happens. All of the teachers gather together in the middle of the corridor, crumple to their knees and shriek in unison, "Make it stop!"

Something about the high-pitched noise is having a powerful effect on them. They squeeze closer and closer together until their bodies merge into one giant wobbling body, with many hands and feet sticking out randomly.

Pupils around you look confused, as if they've just woken from a dream.

"Schools out!" you yell, running for the exit yourself.

THE END

B: You follow Mr Lotcorn and the boy, at a distance

You keep your steps light. Where's Mr Lotcorn taking him and why does the boy look so scared?

The boy starts crying. Mr Lotcorn says, "Assimilation is necessary."

What does he mean? 'Assimilation' – that's taking over something, isn't it? You've watched episodes of Dr. Who and Star Trek. Mr Lotcorn and the boy disappear into the school assembly hall.

You creep up to the hall door and peer inside. Three rows of children stand in lines, like they did this morning to go into class. At the front of each line a teacher holds a large syringe. The syringe is clear and filled with a glowing green liquid.

As each child is jabbed, without a single flinch, they leave the line and stand over to one side. You notice that their eyes start glowing!

What is this? You spin around in a panic, saying to yourself, "Time to get out of here!"

Sprinting down the corridor you get to the fire door at the end. Before you can open it, you sense someone is behind you.

"Come now," a voice says, behind you. Icy fingers creep up your spine.

"You'll feel so much better once you've had your inoculations. So many nasty bugs going around this time of year."

Turning around, you see a tall woman, who looks like a doctor in a white coat, gliding towards you, hovering a few inches above the ground, with a trail of smoking sticky slime behind her.

"You'll soon be one of us!" she lisps, in bizarre multiple voices.

THE END

B: Instead of going to the Headmaster's office, you sneak off to reception and ask for your phone

It's odd being alone in the empty school corridors. You wonder what this place will feel like next week when the school is full. Maybe you'll go to the Headmaster's office later. First, you want to be the one to tell your parents about what just happened, before they hear it from a teacher.

At the main reception area, you say hi to the woman behind the counter. "Could you help me please?"

She looks surprised and rather disturbed to see you. "Why are you out of class?"

"I need to use my phone to call my parents. It's an emergency."

She shakes her head. "I don't think so. That's not permitted. All devices are given back to pupils after the school day has finished."

"Yeah, I heard." You try out your most charming smile. "But this is my first day and I just remembered that I'm supposed to have a doctor's appointment. I need to check the time."

"Sorry, but there are no exceptions. You really should not be wandering around. Wait here and Dr Popeson will escort you back to class."

Dr Popeson comes out of the reception office. "Hello! Your first day is it? Welcome! How do you like it here so far?"

"Fine, I suppose," you reply, shrugging. "It's a bit different to my old school."

"Well, secondary school is a different experience. Come on, I'll take you back to Class X."

"How did you know that's my class?" you ask.

"It's our job to know which children belong in which class," she says, smiling.

"I need to use the toilet."

"No problem. I'll wait for you outside."

This annoys you. I'm not a baby, you think. "That's alright. I'll be fine."

"But it's our policy, leave no one behind!"

Once inside the toilets, you hear whispering. Pushing open each stall door, you see Billie huddled over, clutching a phone, texting a message.

"What are you doing?" you ask, surprised to see Billie.

Billie stares at you and pushes their face right into yours. "You haven't had your jab yet?"

Why is everyone here so weird?!

"No. It's my first day!"

Billie relaxes, and then grabs your arm. "Do you

think this place is a bit odd? That kid bursting in just now? Everything seems really off! I've texted my brother. He's picking me up, but..."

"How did you sneak your phone in? Didn't everyone hand them in?"

"On Monday when they asked for our phones -- it felt like a breach of, you know, our rights? So today I handed over an old phone that's bust and took the battery out of this one and snuck it in my sock. All week, kids have been acting different. I knew some of them really well from primary school, and now they don't recognise me at all!"

"I better go. Dr Popeson's outside waiting to take me back to class."

"Something isn't right here and I'm going to find out what. Help me through this window. My brother will be in the car park in five minutes. Want to come?"

CHOICE: You're the boss! Which do you choose?

A: You crawl out of the window with Billie

(Go to page 132)

B: You go back out to Dr Popeson (Go to page 134)

A: You crawl out of the window with Billie

Squeezing through the window, following Billie, you feel excited, but also fearful.

What are you doing? Your parents had warned you before not to be so suggestible, but Billie is right – something strange is going on, and once you get to the bottom of it, you know your parents will understand.

Landing softly on the grass below, you both run across the playground as fast as you can. You jump over a low brick wall. Standing in front of you is a old, serious-looking woman with her arms folded.

"Hello, children." Her eyes are very dark, almost black. She smiles and licks her lips, her tongue moving like a lizard's. "I'm Dr Nivea."

You gulp.

Dr Nivea grins. A dribble of black oil squeezes out of her lips.

Billie pushes you forward. "Got another one for you, Doctor."

What? You stare open mouthed at Billie, then at Dr. Nivea.

"I thought you said your brother--"

Billie smiles and you notice the same black oil starting to dribble from their lips. "I was an only child. But thanks to Dr Nivea and the others, I'll never be alone again. And neither will you."

Billie stretches out a hand towards you, tentacles dangling, and you scream and scream.

THE END

B: You go back out to Dr Popeson

"What took you so long?" Dr Popeson asks, as you come out of the bathroom.

You decide not to mention Billie's departure through the bathroom window. You figure it's none of your business.

Walking down the corridor together, the teacher stops suddenly and says, "You say it's your first day, yes?"

You nod.

Dr Popeson glances round as if worried that you're both being watched. Leaning into you, she whispers.

"Listen carefully. I'm sorry to have to ask for your help, but we don't have much time."

"Much time for what?" you ask, confused.

"All the Year Seven teachers have been taken over by… by something…" she shakes her head, like she can't believe what's coming from her own mouth. "I'm not sure exactly what's going on, but I think they've been influenced by something."

"Really? What makes you think that?"

"At our inset days last week, all staff had to take an eye examination. Then lesson plans were changed, with this new gaming element introduced, and scheduled inoculations for Year Sevens. The other teachers all started acting differently. I think it had to do with the eye test?"

You think of all the teachers you've met so far, all with bright blue eyes.

Dr Popeson carries on. "I'm colour-blind and all the flashing red and green combinations didn't affect me. I'm trying to mimic their behaviour, be as emotionless as possible, but it's only a matter of time before I'm discovered. So, instead… I'm trying to get as many kids as possible out of here. Each day I've manged to send home a few."

You decide to trust her. "Billie from my class just went out the bathroom window!"

Dr Popeson looks relieved. "Good job you didn't go too – Billie has already been assimilated. Come with me."

With her electronic pass, Dr Popeson opens a set of doors marked 'Staff Only'.

"That will take you to the staff car park and round the corner you'll see a bus stop. Go straight home -- tell your parents school is closed. I'll send out letters confirming everything once I'm sure the coast is clear."

You run across the car park as fast as your legs will carry you.

THE END

B: Keep quiet and investigate later

You have no idea what everyone's doing, so you put up your hand, but Miss Perkulea's eyes are closed. You cough to get her attention.

"It's everyone's favourite session now, gaming! Is there a problem?"

"Yes, Miss," you say. "I don't know how to play these games."

"Of course. Well," she comes over and points at Meera's screen. "Meera is playing a biology-based war game: The Parasite Paradox. Next to her, Billie is on FootureU. You can choose either of those, or the new game MINDZBegone."

You shake your head. "I've never heard of those."

"They have been developed by an educational specialist. Excellent for focus and promoting intellectual cognitive behaviour." She slots a disc into my console and hands you a controller. "Follow the onscreen instructions. It's very easy. Don't forget your VR goggles."

As she looks at you to check you understand, you think you notice something odd about her eyes. They seem to flash from brown to blue for a moment, then back again. It must be a trick of the light. Maybe you need your eyes tested.

"I'm Nik," a low voice behind you whispers. "I like your rucksack."

"Thanks," you say, glancing at the Street Fighter characters printed on the back. It'll be great to get home and play your own games later.

Nik says, "Dhalsim's my favourite Street Fighter character."

You're about to tell Nik what characters you like, when he whispers out of the corner of his mouth. "Miss has hearing like a bat," he giggles. "The hearing of a bat, eyes of a cat and a twitching nose like a rat!"

You stifle a laugh. This kid is... something else!

A low buzzer echoes through the classroom. Miss Perkulea stands and announces, "Recreation time! Off you go."

Nik snorts behind you. Turning round, you grin at the comb jammed into his afro which reminds you of your Dad.

"Get that? Who calls it 'recreation time'?" Nik says. "I'm going to the cafeteria to grab a pattie. Want to come?"

CHOICE: You're the boss. Which do you choose?

A: Head into the playground on your own

(Go to page 138)

B: Go to the cafeteria with Nik (Go to page 145)

A: Head to the playground on your own

Walking across the playground, everyone's already in little groups. You feel sad. Mum promised you wouldn't miss much by joining late, but you're not so sure. Seems that everyone has made friends, apart from you.

Then you see a girl standing still with her eyes squeezed shut, tears rolling down her cheeks. She touches her wet cheeks, opens her eyes and gives a massive grin. Dropping her smile, she glances around, looking worried.

Walking over, you ask, "Hi, everything okay?"

"What?" Startled, she steps back away. "Why-why are you asking that?" She looks you up and down suspiciously. "What do you want?"

You don't want anything! "I saw you from over there." You shrug. "You looked upset."

"Did I?"

"It's tough, isn't it?" you say. "Starting at a new school. I get it."

"I'm fine." She wrinkles her nose. "I'm settling in just... great." She peers at you, staring right into your eyes. She sounds almost defiant. "How about you?"

"It's my first day," you reply.

Suddenly, her expression changes. She grabs your blazer sleeve, pulling you close. "You're new?" she leans close and murmurs. "You've never been here before?"

"Yeah. I had a virus, so I missed the rest of the week."

Her eyes light up. "You haven't even had your first jab yet?"

You remember Meera mentioned that too. "What jab?"

"The new student inoculations and eye tests. Monday we all had the eye tests. Then, class Z had their jabs on Tuesday, Y on Wednesday and X had them yesterday. Today we're due our second dose."

"Like a flu jab?"

"So they say," she whispers. "But judging by how people are acting... I reckon something weird is going on."

Just your luck – to have her latch onto you.

You ask, "What do you think is going on then?"

"It seems as if they're removing our emotions!"

What is she talking about?

CHOICE: You're the boss? Which do you choose?

A: You ask her more about it (Go to page 140)

B: You go to find a teacher to help her, as she seems troubled (Go to page 143)

A: You ask her more about it

"What do you mean, 'removing our emotions'?"

"Look around you! Have you ever seen so many quiet, subdued children in a playground? Nobody's playing football, nobody's laughing. There's basketball hoops and footballs and they're untouched! Most of them may as well be sitting in the classroom. I've got a plan to expose the teachers. If we have an emotional meltdown, overload them, before we get given our second jabs, we might get enough time to get out of here. Everyone else I've tried to talk to seems to be already gone. Like, they're not laughing or crying or anything. But you've not had the eye test or the jab yet. Want to help?"

"Sure," you say. You may as well hang out, you think. You've got nothing to lose, though it'd be nice to catch up with Meera and Billie again. "But what's made you so suspicious?"

"All three classes have had their first dose now and everything is different to earlier in the week. Each time a class has their jab... they come back quieter, like they've had part of their personality removed. After a few days it's really noticeable."

"Maybe they've just settled in?"

"No. Seriously. Watch this." She picks up a basketball that is lying nearby. "Check this out." She throws the ball, and it hurtles into a group of boys across from us.

What is she doing?

The ball hits two boys on the back of their legs, hard. But they don't move, or flinch. Nothing. After five seconds, they both turn around.

"Weird, right?!" she says, nudging you.

Right. And instead of yelling, or coming towards you, the boys look at each other and then wave before turning back as if nothing had happened.

"Copy me," she says. She begins laughing hysterically, and people stare.

"Do something funny!" she hisses.

Like what? People move closer, the louder she laughs. Meera and Billie both look at her curiously, frowning as if trying to remember something. You start doing some stupid dance moves and squawking like a chicken.

It's quiet at first but then ripples of laughter carry across the playground. The kids lose their glassy-eyed stares.

"It's working!" she cries. "Keep going!"

You make more and more stupid moves, throwing in some outdated floss moves for good measure.

Pupils are laughing uncontrollably now, while the

teachers march around trying desperately to order them to be quiet.

Eventually, while all the pupils around you are in tears of laughter, you notice the teachers retreating slowly to a far corner of the playground. One by one, heads lowered, they disappear into a jet-black portal in mid-air.

THE END

B: You go to find a teacher to help her

"Wait right here, I'll be back in a second," you say.

You head across the playground towards a teacher standing by the entrance doors.

"Um, Sir?"

He turns towards you, blinking slowly. There's something odd about his eyes too.

"Yes?" he scratches at his ear. "How can I help you?"

"I think someone needs help."

"Do you now? And who might that be?"

"A girl over there." You point across the playground, but now can't see her anywhere. Where did she go? "A girl was crying."

"Oh, dear," the teacher says, shaking his head. "That doesn't sound good, does it? We can't have that! Many children find starting a new school quite difficult."

You joke to relieve the tension. "Yeh, some kids reckon the best bit about school is the end of day bell!"

His blank expression doesn't change. Then he opens his mouth and says, "Ha, ha, ha."

What had the girl said, about all emotion being removed? Was she right?

"I see no crying girl. Breaktime is over. Now, time for everyone's final jabs."

He grabs your arm so tightly that it hurts.

"Sir!"

He pulls you along and your feet lift off the ground. You remember the boy being dragged out of your classroom earlier...

"Help!" you scream as you're dragged past other teachers crowded round the entrance doors.

No-one looks at you.

"We need to give this one his injection immediately," one says. "A double dose. The girl is having hers as we speak."

As you're dragged to the assembly hall, you see the girl walking towards you quietly, next to another teacher.

"What happened?" you ask anxiously. "Are you okay?"

"I'm fine," she murmurs peacefully, staring straight ahead. "Everything's going to be just fine."

THE END

B: Go to the cafeteria with Nik

The school cafeteria is huge, but with only the Year Sevens here it doesn't look too busy. Groups of children sit together, but they aren't speaking, just eating their snacks almost likc robots.

"What's up with everyone in this place?" you ask Nik. "It's so... quiet."

"Yeah, a few of that lot," Nik points to a couple of tables, "they used to be my friends and went to my primary school. At the start of the week we got on, but then they started acting distant. Maybe just because we're in different classes now? I dunno."

You join the back of a line for the vending machine.

"Have you got your jab after lunch?" Nik asks.

You nod. "Yeah, that's what my timetable says. Is it alright?"

"It doesn't hurt much. Our class got the first dose yesterday. We were the last class to get it." Nik scratches his head. "I have been feeling a bit weird though."

"Weird how?" you ask.

Before he answers, there's a huge commotion at the back of the cafeteria. Someone laughs hysterically. You turn around and see Meera stood on the table. As two teachers try to grab her, she dodges their grasp and starts throwing food at them.

"You can't stop me laughing if I'm happy!" she yells. "You can't control me!"

"What the heck?" You stare at her, about to burst into laughter yourself. This was not how you expected your first day at a new school to go!

"Get out while you can!" she screeches to the people staring at her. "We're okay. We can still beat them. It's not too late!"

"That is enough of that behaviour." A teacher says, seizing Meera and throwing her over his shoulder. "This type of behaviour is unacceptable!" He marches out to the kitchen with her.

Hardly anyone blinks an eye. Everyone goes back to eating, just like before, when that boy burst into your classroom.

Something's definitely not right! You turn to Nik. "What's wrong with them all? Where are they taking Meera?"

"Who knows?" says Nik. "Let's get out of here!"

CHOICE: You're the boss. Do you:

A: Leave the cafeteria with Nik (Go to page 149)

B: Follow the teacher who took Meera (Go to page 147)

B: Follow the teacher who took Meera

You walk through into the school kitchen, but no-one's there. A door at the back swings open. Going through it leads to a car park. Where's Meera?

In front of you is a huge... spaceship. There's no other word for it. Unless this is just an art project or gigantic drama prop? You gaze up at the massive structure, mouth hanging open.

A silver ramp leads to an opening. You duck forward, seeing if you can peer inside without stepping closer. "Meera?" you call.

"Meera will be fine!" A voice booms out. "What's so bad about being a part of something?"

The teacher who carried Meera off comes down the ramp. He's holding either side of his head as if he's afraid it might fall off.

"Really. You know your planet is doomed, don't you? You humans have been given many years and opportunities to fix things. But still you consume as if tomorrow will never arrive. Buying new, not recycling, global warming, overpopulation, environmental damage beyond repair, sea levels rising -- using all your resources: need I go on? Join us! We have the technology to fix your dying planet. All we ask is for an equal partnership."

You can't believe what you're hearing. "Wh-what do you want? Where's Meera?"

"She's on board, having a top-up jab. We need a young population, bodies which haven't been damaged or worn out. Energetic souls who can't regulate their emotions. Your energy keeps us going. Small price to pay, isn't it?"

"But... why are you killing us?"

He laughed. "We aren't killing you! We remove excess emotion and replace it with logic. Technological advances cannot be made when emotions run so high. People are either too happy to want to work, or they become sad, bored, or angry – then they make silly mistakes. You'll soon be one of us."

Bringing a large syringe from behind his back, he's by your side in an instant.

THE END

A: Leave the cafeteria with Nik

Nik says, "I know where we can find some answers, maybe."

"Where?" you ask.

"The staff room!"

You and Nik head down a corridor. Nik takes different turnings, eventually reaching a white door marked Staff Only.

You both push on the door hard and it swings open. You both walk through it and the door slams shut behind you. You blink, blinded by sunshine.

"There's no handle!" Nik wails.

Where are you? A moment ago you were both in a school corridor but now...

You take in your surroundings. This isn't the school grounds! You don't recognise anything.

"Why is it so hot?" Nik asks, pulling at his collar. "I'm thirsty."

It's boiling. You can barely take a breath, the air is so dry. The sky is blue and vast.

Nik starts crying. "Is this even England?" On his knees, he starts banging at the closed door. "Help us!" he shouts.

In front of you are palm trees heavy with... are those coconuts?

It's a beautiful landscape, but there's no doubt about it – you're trapped. One long dusty lane is in front of you, and there's nothing else as far as the eye can see.

"Maybe we'll find something at the end of the road?" you say. Nik shakes his head, snivelling. "I'm not going anywhere. Someone will come by, someone will open this door!"

You don't think so. You take off your blazer and tie it around your waist. You take off your tie and unbutton your top button. Looks like you've got a long walk ahead. To where? Somewhere.

THE END

START AGAIN

GAME OVER

PLAY AGAIN

ONCE

CLARE WEZE
ILLUSTRATED BY CAMILLA RU

We'd been practising flying for weeks before it happened. Every day after school, Elise called round for me and we'd race through the lonely spinney behind our houses and on up the steep hillside with our wings – old sheets stitched to half a hula hoop each.

That session started the same as all the others. As always we took off together, launching skyward, thinking of faraway places. And as always, the air stayed thin and down I crashed, but this time, Elise just... didn't. For three incredible seconds, she actually flew.

'You flew!'

We stood gaping at each other. Elise's wings were droopy and shaky. My heart hammered fast – I think I'd forgotten to breathe. Then I grabbed both her arms and shrieked, 'Elise – you did it! You really did it!'

She nodded, still too shocked to speak. I let go of her and started jumping up and down and she copied me, and we jumped there together, laughing and whooping.

'Hey,' Elise said. 'When we get it totally perfect, we can go exploring–'

'Yeah, we'd have to be quick, though, and really careful so nobody sees us.'

'Whoa – maybe we could even get camouflaged up!' she said. 'Then we could absolutely and totally travel.'

I pictured us up there. Not too high, but high enough to use the wind, to ride it like we'd always dreamed we would. 'Never believed we'd actually do it,' I said, and another shudder of shock went through me. 'You should try it again. Exactly the same.'

She nodded and kept her eyes on mine while she raised her arms and tried to focus, breathing like she was blowing up a balloon.

'Quick!' I said, and she jumped – and dropped. 'Oh,' she said, and tried again. 'It's not working.'

She went again. And again. Fifteen times. I analysed each one, shouting instructions:

'Arms higher!'

'Jump stronger!'

My turn came, and the shakes took over again. I felt like I was falling upwards. My breathing was quivery. My heart beat so fast it nearly toppled me over. I leapt into the air, flapped my wings, and landed in a heap.

Elise said, 'You're doing it wrong, Kayla. Keep your arms out strong. Don't flap too soon.'

I tried again and again. My braids smacked my cheeks over and over, almost hitting me in the eye, but I kept going.

'Watch out!' Elise yelled. 'You're over the muddy bit!'

We carried on leaping, together and separately, any and every way we could think of. Our arms and legs ached but we kept going until we collapsed on the spongy, mossy grass to nurse bashed knees. Normally we focused only on each other and the flying, but now I felt, saw and heard everything going on around us. Every thistle. Every dandelion-head. Any and all of it could be part of the secret. A little bird flying high – that could have been a witness. The spell was broken by three jackdaws walking the field behind us, like old men looking for something – looking hard – and taking no notice of us whatsoever. If only we could ask them for tips.

'How'd it feel?' I asked her.

'Like swimming. Normal. Easy.'

'Not like when the wind lifts us?'

'No,' she said, getting up again. 'Completely different.' Her strong, tennis-player's hands danced along the edges of her wings after she'd hitched them over her shoulders, back and forth, willing them to cooperate. 'And it isn't all that windy today.'

She was right. It wasn't. 'You looked delicate,' I said.

Her face went dreamy again. 'Like a bird?'

'No. Light, like a butterfly.'

I was the gangly one. Elise was shorter, stronger. She tried again then got annoyed with it all, stomping down the hill a little way and back to me in a cross rectangle, even kicking, until I could smell the bruising on the grass she savaged. A startled bird shot straight up into the sky shrieking the alarm.

'Stop it!' I said. 'Not like that.' When she'd flown, silence had hung in the air like something solid; I knew that much. We might even have breathed it in along with the air. 'Be delicate, like before. Be graceful. You were so graceful.'

'I'm trying to remember,' she said. Her voice was getting growly and low. It always did that when she was frazzled.

She tried again, but everything went wrong and after her crash she looked as if she'd been planted into the ground. She might sprout. I smothered a giggle. 'Your bunches have caught grass seeds.'

But Elise wasn't interested. 'Look at that!' she said. Far

below us, the grey misty stuff that had been hanging over the town all day had gathered over our row of houses. You couldn't see the spinney at all. 'A cloud has literally fallen!'

Soon that cloud would creep up the hill and we'd have to go in for tea and homework, Elise to her house and me to mine four doors along. I had a feeling that once the sun went down on today – a day that held a moment of flying – that would be it. The barrier was like a wall of glass so fine you'd never even be able to feel it. And there weren't many weeks left before she'd start at the grammar school fifteen miles away and I wouldn't.

Elise must have been thinking the same kind of thing, because when the whole sky darkened and the wind got up, she didn't get ready to pack up and go. She carried on trying.

'It's going to rain,' I said, plucking more grass to tear up. I was always tearing grass. I loved the smell. 'Come on.'

'Not yet.'

She wouldn't come no matter what I said, so ran down into the gloom by myself, and we still both got drenched. She caught up with me in the spinney, pulling wet trousers away from each leg with both hands.

'Kayla! You left me!'

'Well you wouldn't come!'

Something a little bit fiery and dangerous fizzed between us.

At home, Mum told me it was probably just that Elise was worrying about starting at a new school that had nobody else she knew, and the nerves were bubbling over into snappishness, but my throat felt tight and wrong. I already knew all that. Elise didn't talk about the grammar school, but I'd counted the days we had left. One more week of school, six weeks of school holidays, and then she'd be gone. But we'd still have every evening together, and weekends. Wouldn't we?

'Saw you playing up there,' Mum said. 'You looked to be getting on fine.'

'We weren't playing. We were practising flying.'

'Aw, cute! All that leaping and tumbling! Great exercise.'

I rolled my eyes at her, and at the noodles she was spooning out. 'Mum, Elise flew.'

Mum frowned and blinked and stopped spooning.

'She actually flew,' I said. 'I saw her.'

'But Kayla, that's ...' Mum looked like she wanted to laugh but was fighting it. 'It's lovely that you still think you can fly.' She put the spoon and pan down and squeezed my shoulder. 'When I was your age, I used to dream about finding the end of the rainbow. I can't imagine a thermal lifting anyone from that height, but ... Do you know what a thermal is? It's rising air. Birds glide on thermals–'

'It wasn't air. It wasn't the wind. She really did fly. Just for a couple of seconds.'

*

The next day – a Saturday – we tried again, this time with sandwiches, fruit and drinks for lunch. Our flights started out with loads of pep, but it didn't take long before they were just useless and painful again.

'We need to get rid of this gap,' Elise said. Her hands curved over the hula-hoop, pulling the sheet tight. 'There shouldn't be a gap where air can leak out. We should be like bats.'

'Or birds?'

'No,' she said. 'Bats. Birds are different.'

'How?'

'Feathers are complicated,' she said. 'Bats match us better.'

'You've been reading about it,' I said, crushing more grass between my fingers.

She ignored that and said, 'People aren't believing us, you know.'

'I know! My mum had such a look on her face! Like we were babies, making it up. Playing.'

Elise nodded. 'Same. My brother. And my dad. They're

such dingbats. They don't know anything. Asher told me the only way we're ever going to do it is to get a hang glider.'

Her bossy brother Asher just would say that. I pictured how his face had probably looked while he said it – eyes screwed up, nose high so he could look down it and laugh – but not his hair, because every time you saw him, her brother had changed his hairstyle.

'Let's come up here tonight,' Elise said.

'Tonight?'

'Yeah. There's more wind at night. That'll lift us up, and whatever made me fly yesterday will catch hold then, and keep us up.'

'No way…'

'Kayla, yes, it'll be fine!'

I shook my head. 'I'd never be allowed and if I tried to sneak out I'd be caught …'

'Why would you? You can just–'

'Anyway, if it's so windy, we might get blown away,' I said, and carried on shaking my head in a way she'd know was absolutely final. The. End. 'Blowing away isn't flying.'

Elise glared at me.

*

Late that night I looked out of my bedroom window. The spinney and the hill beyond were a whole different world at night. Elise was right, the wind was strong. It looked scary. You wouldn't want to be out there.

Then a cloud drifted across the sky, revealing the moon, and now everything looked mysterious but beautiful, too. Almost inviting. Maybe Elise was right—

A figure climbed the hill. Small, with flappy parts and a tiny light. Elise! All by herself. I dived for my clothes and crept out of the house.

It was horrible in the spinney on my own in the dark. The moonlight was strong enough to see quite a lot. Too much. My shadow went first, and that felt as spooky as the looming branches, if that's what they were. Some of them could have been fingers reaching out – that's how bad the spinney is for your imagination.

At the other side I legged it, not daring to shout out to Elise in case Mum heard me. By the time I reached her my lungs felt ready to burst and my legs were killing me.

'Elise!'

She jumped – almost totally out of her skin – and dropped her torch. 'Oh my God, you – arghh! I nearly died of shock!'

But she was grinning her head off, and when we started flying we were giddy goats, bouncing with the excitement and badness of being out after dark, scaring each other, loving it.

'Yaaay!' I screamed.

'Dark flying wins it!'

The wind helped. It added a bit of slow-mo before we hit the ground, and the thrill and rush of its power gave us zing. We were so utterly energised. We could do anything. Someone could have given us a great big problem in the world – like climate change – and we'd have solved it in five minutes. The car lights in town below looked like golden fish eyes weaving in and out – pretty, but feeble compared to us.

Then I slammed down hard, winded myself and somersaulted down the hill. Had to stop myself with my bare palms. Elise's giggles made it hurt a bit less.

I rested on the damp grass. The air smelt so different at night. The moon made ordinary things look elongated and otherworldly. The clouds that skimmed across it were jagged, their undersides shining like slivers of frozen lightning. Elise had set her torch on the ground at an angle, and it made clumps of nettles look like cowering wolves that knew something we didn't.

Elise kept at it, madly now. Her legs did scissor kicks as if she was already up there. One of her leaps was so huge. My heart was in my mouth – please land softly – but she crashed hard. She landed with the sheeting in a knot.

'Elise! Oh, I wish you'd stop it now – I'm scared you'll break your ankle, or something.'

'We need to bring a stool up here,' she said, 'or a step to make a little ledge to take off from.'

I pointed to the slope we sat on. 'A stool? It would fall over.'

She breathed out a long, deep drained sigh. 'We could cut out a chunk of hill or dig the back legs into it. Definitely,' she said, but her voice was slowing down. 'It's what's missing.'

I sighed too. We'd calmed right down into lullaby land. Trying and failing again and again stopped mattering when the moon looked like a film moon. When there were just a handful of stars looking like stars from a fairy tale, and you could easily imagine taking off, gliding closer to them and just hanging silently up there before swooping back to earth like an owl. How cold would it be up there?

In the moonlight, Elise looked like she was hardly breathing. Her serious face was as still as a painting. 'All our lawns look like patchwork that someone's done on purpose,' she said softly. 'To make a pattern that you only see properly from up here.'

I squinted at the place where I thought my bedroom should be, but it was just a dark dot.

And then a ripple of wind went right through the grass

next to us, like something alive. It was time to go.

'We'll hold hands through the spinney,' Elise said. 'Then I'll go through your garden and out to the front where the street lights are. I'll go home that way.'

But then, like a nightmare, a shadow broke away from the darkness of the spinney and started moving up the hill towards us. Rapidly. My heart beat so hard I could feel the throbbing in my toes. The shadow had no torch, so couldn't possibly be a person. In the seconds I had, my brain invented every type of monster.

There came a point where the monster looked like Mum – it had her bantu-knotted hair – but my brain wouldn't let go of the fear. My breathing was ragged and strangled, right up until she said,

'I was going to ring the police until I saw your torch, Elise. You ridiculous pair! What on earth were you thinking?'

We took Elise right to her door. When we got home, there was a long talk about always going to her first with any decision, and that next time I went to Dad's, she would expect me to confess to him. In person.

*

Day Three. Elise brought shiny new fabric to our hillside and attached it to her hula hoop with a staple gun she'd pinched from her brother's room.

'They need to be like membranes,' she said.

I let the fabric slide between my fingers. 'Where d'you get this?'

'Mum was going to use it to cover the garden table, but it isn't properly waterproof so she let me have it. I'll test it out, then if it works, I'll redo yours.'

I don't know what made me say it, but this was what I blurted next: 'Maybe it's nothing to do with the equipment. Maybe it was just that one time.'

This had been nagging at the corners of my mind ever since Elise flew, but her eyes went dark. Her lips tightened. She stood up to fly without speaking.

This new flight attempt was much worse than with the sheets. Her arms were stiff and couldn't flap properly. It was like a sheep's jump – it got her into the air, but then: splat.

'Ouch!' I said, to fill in the silence, but it was no good. It felt like she'd never speak again. She ripped the shiny fabric from the hula hoops and remade the sheet wings with the kind of fury I've only seen in films. Her face was hot. I could see it – sweat shone on her forehead and her cheeks were pinkish. All her movements were fast and sharp, like she was made out of fuming sewing machines. Even the plastic hoop made an angry clicking noise against her fingernails.

Then suddenly she stood up, shrugged on the wings and said, 'I'm off. Gonna try it over there.' She looked towards the top of our hill and curved her hand over.

'What, right over the other side?'

She nodded.

'But ...'

We never went over the other side of the hill, because neither of us were allowed out of sight of our houses. It was OUT: out of the question, out of bounds, out of hand. Something had happened over that hill sometime back in the day, maybe even before we were born. Something nobody talked about, something made out of rumours and whispers. Some of the kids at our school pretend it's haunted.

'I can't go there,' I said. I wasn't about to do something else illegal just because Elise wanted it.

Elise put her finger to her lips. 'Promise not to tell on me?'

I nodded slowly. 'OK. But don't do it, though!'

She ignored that and raced off, disappearing over the edge before I'd had time to believe she really would.

And then I was alone. The only sounds were crows cawing, and far-away traffic. I didn't move for a few minutes. Couldn't. And then I stood up and took a few steps after her.

'Elise!'

It was just one long shout, but it was very, very loud. There was no answer.

Without wanting to at all, I climbed to the top of the hill too, and looked over the edge, heart thumping at what I'd never seen before: a grassy hill – the mirror of the one on our side – ending in thick dark woods straight out of a fairy tale. Beyond that, countryside rolled away in every direction. And no Elise.

*

She didn't come back. I waited at the top, on the very edge of where I was allowed to be. I shouted twice more, but she'd disappeared into thin air. My voice echoed down into those trees and their shadows like an alarm, one that might attract things I didn't want to think about. Waiting felt unreal, like a dream. I felt lost in it, as if waiting was an actual place and I couldn't escape.

Somehow I snapped out of it and pelted down the hill, snatching up the wings I'd abandoned on the way.

Elise's house always had its own smell: glue, boiled pasta, herbs. A bit of paint. On top of all that today, there was a strong smell of cooking that wafted right from the back gate. I hadn't stopped running all the way there. Asher came to the door, and after I'd panted, gulped and heaved out the problem, he took over, just like a policeman.

'We'll find her. Go home. You've done the right thing reporting this.' He always towered over me but loomed especially tall today.

'But–'

'Go home, Kayla.'

*

Mum went round three times. Elise had run away, they thought.

'It's probably all about the new school,' Mum said. 'Maybe she really didn't want to go after all.'

'She wouldn't do that without telling me. It doesn't make sense.'

Mum had me sleeping in her bed to prevent me from joining the search. Not much sleep was had by either of us. Probably not by anyone at Elise's house either. I lay there and imagined Elise lost forever, like Kay in The Snow Queen. Mum sighed and turned over every time I wriggled, but I couldn't help it.

Elise wasn't found until the next morning. She missed

a whole day of school with all the fuss, and was found wandering on the fast road out of town, bedraggled and upset. Mum reported the news in short, gentle sentences, like I was a baby. She saved the ultimate bombshell for last: Elise and her family were moving to a village way beyond the other side of town. We weren't just going to have separate schools; we were going to separate completely.

'That's why she's been so skittish with you,' Mum said. 'Poor little love. So unsettling for her.'

Which sent me running round to Elise's house to say: 'Why didn't you tell me you were moving?' I was breathing hard. I was mad.

'You told on me. I asked you not to tell anyone and as soon as I'd gone over that hill, you couldn't wait to snitch–'

'I did wait! I stayed there ages, but you didn't come back!'

'But you said. You promised.'

My mouth dried out suddenly. 'I only wanted to make sure you didn't get hurt–'

'Your promise was a lie. You lied when you said you wouldn't tell. You're a liar.'

'I am not!' I leapt for her, arms out, fingers scrabbling to scratch. I wouldn't have scratched her – I really wouldn't. I stopped well before I reached her, but she took a step back as if I was dangerous and gross. She looked at me with such things in her eyes – shock, hurt, dislike – and after that, the nastiness between us seemed to drag us under. It ran away with us, like we weren't even doing this ourselves.

I turned away and walked towards home without looking back, but once there, I felt sick. Sicker than when I ate an egg sandwich that was off. Far sicker.

*

Days went by and nothing changed. There was no Elise. Mum didn't ask me anything.

The school holidays began. I went clothes shopping with Mum. We made stakes for the garden vegetables and picked all the raspberries together. She didn't ask what was wrong, so I couldn't say 'nothing'. She didn't ask where Elise was. She just made all my favourite dinners, and studied me when she thought I wasn't looking.

I watched all the films I could find, every programme, listened to every piece of music I had and went to three holiday club sessions, but nothing was any fun. Most things tasted, felt or sounded hollow.

Two weeks of the holidays disappeared down a hole.

I couldn't sit around any longer, so I started gluing small

paper models of the two of us flying. I gave us delicate net wings cut from an old lilac jewellery bag, wings that would never have held us up in real life. I like to seal important things, and this is how I do it. It helps me understand. And Elise writes things down, always with pen top monsters on her pens. She'd have pages and pages of notes about the flying – I just knew it. I pictured her writing about us now, monsters quivering.

Writing about her flight.

Writing down her thoughts.

When I'd used up all the glue and got the model as perfect as possible, I sat with my chin in my hands, closed my eyes, and thought about flying, and Elise, and the first day of Reception class together. I thought about her tennis club and my art club and her writing and my modelling.

Everything came back to that flight. Elise lifting off. Elise staying in the air. How, just how? And why? It couldn't have been magic or imagination, because Elise did it and we both saw it. Imagination doesn't work like that. And I don't think magic is real. The flying was something soft and hard to get hold of – like dust, or a thought – but it was real.

And I knew what Elise was thinking. I knew her so well. She'd be thinking that flying wasn't the impossible thing – it couldn't be, because she'd done it. Not being able to fly again when you've proved it once – that was the impossible part. That's what was so maddening for her. And for me.

I got a piece of cream-coloured paper with gold edges and wrote that down. And next to it, I wrote:

Maybe we were trying too hard. You weren't even trying when it happened. We were just enjoying ourselves. We need to relax. We need to stop trying.

I took a picture of my model and printed it out. I drew a little picture on the note too, of us flying together over fields of long grasses that waved like a gentle sea. Next to the picture, I wrote:

Sorry.

Elise would be amazed. Writing isn't my thing.

*

Delivering the envelope was harder. I had to get it through her letter box and go away without being seen. There were so many chances of being caught: opening her gate; darting down her path; turning around and doing it all in reverse. My stomach was a jelly.

In the end, her mum came to the door as I was opening the gate. 'Kayla! We've missed you.'

Asher appeared in the window for a second, then vanished,

and my tongue refused to work. I smiled at their mother, handed over the envelope with Elise's name on, failed to utter a single word to her and walked away like someone strange.

*

I thought it would be awkward and stiff when we got back together, but it wasn't. It was just like nothing had happened. We smiled at the same time. We grabbed our wings and scrambled up the hill, and every breath I took seemed to fill me with more energy.

We stood in our places and looked down at the seagulls looping over the roofs of our houses.

Elise said: 'I'll miss living at the very edge of town.'

I didn't ask: What did you do at other side of the hill? Instead, I said, 'We don't ever need to let anything separate us ever again.'

Shc shook her head vigorously. 'Nothing. Ever. Not the grammar school. Not stupid new houses.'

'You might like it,' I said. 'It might be an awesome house!'

She smiled sadly.

'I can't wait to see it,' I said.

She grinned and said, 'Let's try again. One more session!' and we did, through giggles, and the giggling took us back to the beginning of summer, and then to last summer, and even the one before that. All our crazy times.

We tried three brand new take-offs, one of them backwards, and one of them leaning-falling. None of them worked. It didn't matter.

Eventually the laughter took all our strength away and we sank to our knees while our breath caught up.

'You did fly,' I told her.

We smiled at each other for a long time, then lay back and watched the sky for wing-beats.

ASHER IS A ROCKSTAR!

DEAN ATTA
ILLUSTRATED BY OLIVIA TWIST

PART 1: RUBEN SAYS 'YES'

Asher Tembo is my best friend
and Asher is a rock star.

She is the coolest, most talented,
most amazing person I know.

She isn't a celebrity;
she doesn't have songs on the radio,
she hasn't been on TV,
she hasn't made a music video
and she hasn't gone viral online.

When I say Asher is a rock star,
I mean she's a rock star in my eyes.

My name is Josh Appiah,
I'm ten years old and I'm from Brixton,
which is in South London.

My best friend, Asher, is eleven.
Asher has always been
and will always be exactly
one year older than me
because we have the same birthday.

We have joint parties
at the church hall. Everyone comes;
family, friends from church
and friends from school.

We go to different schools
but we see each other all the time;
on Sundays at church
and in the school holidays
at church holiday club.

Holiday club is really fun
and the meals are awesome.
We're allowed seconds,
which mum can't usually
afford to give me at home.

If Asher goes away on holiday,
she sends postcards with poems
she writes especially for me.

This one was from Barcelona:

> 'I really miss you, my best friend.
> I can't wait for this holiday to end.
> Spain is too hot but the food is nice.
> Paella is like Spanish jollof rice.
> I hope you're enjoying holiday club.
> I know how much you love the grub.

You always go for a second plate.
Your amazing appetite is so great!'

I've never been away on a holiday.
I've never been on a plane to Spain,
a ferry to France or a train to Scotland.
Asher has been to all of those countries,
just like a rock star on a world tour!

The main reason Asher is a rock star
is because Asher plays electric guitar.
We both play in the church band.
Our biggest fan is my brother Ruben.

Ruben is fifteen. He's nonverbal,
which means he doesn't speak.

He has a Yes/No button communication device,
which means you ask questions
to find out what he wants,
what he likes and doesn't like.

When we play, Ruben says, 'Yes yes yes'

It feels great when Ruben does this
because he's telling us he's happy.

I play clarinet. I want a saxophone
but Mum can't afford to buy me one.

When I'm older and I have a job
I'll be able to buy one for myself.

Our vicar, Father Francis,
loaned me a clarinet from church.
He said it's on the condition
I play in the church band every Sunday.

Father Francis is from Nigeria.
He lived there before moving here.

Mum is from Ghana
but I've never been there.

Asher's parents are from Zimbabwe
but she's not been there, either.

Father Francis's sermons are about love,
acceptance and forgiveness.

Asher is very forgiving.
When people call Asher 'he',
I tell them, 'The correct pronoun is she.'

Asher says, 'It's okay, they didn't know.'
But sometimes it's people who do know.

Asher is transgender.
That's another reason Asher is a rock star.

Sometimes strangers stare at her
and it's like she's already a celebrity.

I think Asher will be famous one day.
Father Francis does, too.

Father Francis told Asher,
'You glorify God when you use the gifts
He gave you. You walk in your truth
and Jesus walks with you.'

We play hymns in church band
but Asher also writes her own songs.
They're catchy and easy for me
to learn the melody on clarinet.
Asher wrote this song about Ruben.
When we play it for him, he always joins in.

Ruben Says 'Yes'
You look stressed
when you see me in a dress
but Ruben says, 'Yes yes yes yes yes'

Pink nail polish on,
my hair freshly pressed
and Ruben says, 'Yes yes yes yes yes'

I'll never say 'No'
to being my best
when Ruben says,'Yes yes yes yes yes'

Am I a rock star?
Are you obsessed?
Ask Ruben. He says, 'Yes yes yes'

PART 2: TICK TOCK

Ruben is outgrowing his wheelchair.
Mum wants to do an online fundraiser
for a new one. When Mum asks Ruben
if that would be okay, he says, 'No'

When Asher and I ask Ruben
if we can do a fundraising concert
for him, he doesn't answer
right away but then he says, 'Yes'

Asher and I both jump for joy.
'We better get rehearsing,' says Asher.
Then she asks my mum, 'Aunty,
can Josh come to my house to rehearse?'

Even though we're not related
Asher calls my mum Aunty
and I call Asher's parents Aunty and Uncle.
It's just the polite thing to say.

Asher's house is only a few streets away
but it's like another world.

They have a spare bedroom,
which is where I sleep when I stay the night.

It's always strange to be by myself.

At home I share a room with Ruben
and sometimes Mum comes in
to check on him at night.

Our home doesn't have any stairs
but Asher's has two flights
because it's got three floors.
The top floor is just for Aunty and Uncle.

The middle floor has Asher's room,
the guest room and a bathroom.
The ground floor has the living room,
dining room, kitchen and another toilet.

Most importantly, they have a massive garden
with swings and our music shed
where we rehearse Asher's songs,
so we don't disturb Aunty and Uncle.

Asher has decorated the walls
with pictures of her favourite musicians:
Jimi Hendricks, Lenny Kravitz,
Brittany Howard and Prince.

There are hundreds of fairy lights in here,
a heater for when it's cold
and an amplifier for Asher's guitar.
Asher has named her guitar Minty.
Minty has a mint green body,
white pick guard, brown neck and head.
Asher got it for her last birthday
and returned the church guitar.

I haven't named my clarinet
because it's not really mine, it's borrowed.
One day, when I have a saxophone
I'm going to name it Monty.

I take my clarinet out of its case
and put the five pieces together,
mouthpiece, barrel, upper tube,
lower tube and bell. I do like it.

It's black and silver colours are cool
but I dream of having a gold saxophone
to play like Charlie Parker, John Coltrane,
Kamasi Washington and Nubya Garcia.

'What shall we rehearse first?'
Asher asks, holding Minty ready to play.

'We don't have much time today,'
I reply, 'so how about "Tick Tock"?'

Tick Tock
You ask me where I'm from
But not where I'm going:
To the top to the top to the top top top

You tell me to slow down
But I'm never slowing:
Non-stop non-stop non-stop stop stop

Each second on the clock
My confidence is growing:
Tick tock tick tock tick tock tock tock

PART 3: HEADLINERS

The concert will be in the church hall.
The church band are going to play
and some of their professional
musician friends ask to play as well.

We show Ruben videos of the musicians
who offered to play and he picks
the line-up and the running order.
Ruben wants Asher and I to be headliners.

Headliners are the final performers.
This feels like a lot of pressure to me
but Asher doesn't seem nervous at all.
That's another reason she's a rockstar.

But one performer isn't happy
when we send out the running order.
It's not one of the professionals.
It's Tara. She's twelve and sings solos
in church choir.

Before church, Tara comes up to me
and says, 'It's not fair you get to be headliners
just because Ruben is your brother.
Everyone knows I'm a better singer.'

Asher isn't here but I don't answer Tara.
I continue to put my clarinet together:
mouthpiece, barrel, upper tube,
lower tube and bell. I click the case shut.

'Answer me,' says Tara, stomping her foot.

'I didn't hear a question,' I reply, finally
looking up and looking Tara in the eyes.
They shimmer with purple eye shadow.
Her braids have cowrie shells in them this week.

'Who is the better singer, Asher or me?'

'Probably you,' I say to Tara
'but Ruben picked me and Asher
to be headliners. Organise your own
concert, if you're so bothered.'

Tara crosses her arms and narrows
her eyes at me before she says,
'Fine, I'll perform. For Ruben.
Because I'm a good Christian.'
Tara smiles really strangely:
'I just wanted to hear you admit
I'm a better singer than Asher.'

As Tara walks away, she says:
'Hi Asher, I didn't see you there.'

I turn to face my best friend,
who is wearing a light green and blue
flowery dress with a navy bow
around the middle.

She has one hand on her waist,
the other is holding her guitar case.

Her hair is perfectly straightened,
and so is the expression on her face.
Asher stares at me, blankly.

I feel so guilty for saying that
Tara is a better singer than Asher.

'I'm so sorry, Asher,' I say.

She shrugs and smiles,
'Don't be sorry for telling the truth.
Tara is a better singer
but this isn't a competition.
It's a fundraising concert.'

During Father Francis's service,
I wonder if what I said hurt Asher
and she's just acting like it didn't?
I pray to God that she'll forgive me.

After all, Asher is very forgiving.

After church, we make posters
and flyers that say "Rock for Ruben!
Fundraiser for a new wheelchair"
and put them up everywhere.

We rehearse for the concert every day
after school and all day Saturday.
On Sunday we play in church as usual.
That's our routine for three weeks.

We don't speak about what I said.

PART 4: WHO YOU SAY I AM

I think Ruben's concert will be
like one of our birthday parties;
with family, friends from church,
and friends from school. But it isn't!

There are people we don't know here
because they don't need an invitation,
they each pay five pounds to come in.

'I'm so proud of you both,' says Father Francis.

'We haven't played yet,' says Asher,
putting her guitar strap over her shoulder.

Her hair is combed out into a big afro,
she's wearing a black t-shirt,
black leather jacket, black tutu
with leggings and black boots.

'You've brought so many people to church,'
says Father Francis, smiling.

I correct him, 'This isn't church,
it's the church hall.'

Father Francis laughs and says,
'The Church isn't just one building.'

I think of our music shed.
Is it part of Asher's house or not?
It must be. It's in the garden
and the garden is part of the house.

The professional musicians play
and the audience dance and cheer.
I don't dance or cheer because
I'm getting more and more nervous.

I don't want to play. I want to run away
but I know Asher will make everything okay.
She's always so confident.
I look for Asher, who was beside me.

She isn't beside me anymore.

I hear Father Francis introduce Tara,
which means Asher and I are next.
I only have five minutes to find Asher.

I peak out from the side of the stage
into the packed audience.

Everyone is mesmerised by Tara
as she begins singing
"Who You Say I Am" by Hillsong Worship.

There's no sign of Asher's afro anywhere
in the crowd. I have to keep looking.

Asher isn't in the queue for the toilet
but I have a feeling she might be inside,
so I knock on the door.

When the door opens,
it isn't Asher who comes out.

I feel a bit embarrassed
but mostly I feel determined
to find Asher.

Children aren't allowed in the kitchen
but I put my head around the door anyway,
it smells of delicious peanut stew
and is full of aunties talking and laughing
but there's no sign of Asher in here.

I look in the next room
where there are stacks of chairs
and shelves of bibles
but no Asher in here, either.

I return to the back of the stage
and Asher is there.

She's hugging Minty, tightly.

'Where have you been?' I ask,
hoping she'll explain her disappearance
and say something to reassure me.

Asher shakes her head.
'I can't do it,' she says.

'What do you mean?' I ask.
'You're the most confident person I know,'
I say to Asher because it's a fact.

Asher says, 'I feel confident in church,
where most people are friendly.
I've never played to strangers.
What if they stare at me or whisper
the way people in the street do?'

I notice when that happens
but I never knew Asher cared
who whispered or stared.

I try to think of something to say.
Asher is biting her mint green fingernails,
freshly painted to match Minty.

'Asher, you're a rockstar!
You're the coolest, most talented,
most amazing person I know.'

Asher has a look of surprise
and in that moment I realise
I've never told her this before.
She looks down at the floor.

I think I've said something wrong.
When Asher looks up, there are tears
in her eyes and I'm about to apologise
if what I said upset her somehow.

She says, 'Wow! Is that really true?
Josh, I think you're a rockstar too!'

But this sounds so silly to me.

'How can I be a rock star?' I ask.
'I don't play a cool instrument.
I don't even dress cool, like you.'

'Being a rock star isn't about that.
It's not about clothes or instruments
it's about attitude and confidence.'

'I'm not that confident though,
I get my confidence from you.'

'How can that be true, when
I get my confidence from you?'

'How?' I ask, totally confused.

'The way you correct people
when they get my pronouns wrong.
The way you made this
big concert happen for Ruben.
The way you're the youngest
musician in the church band.
'Don't you see how cool you are?'

I'm startled by an eruption of applause.

I realise the audience are clapping
for Tara, which means it's our turn.

Father Francis is back on stage:
'Now, it's time for our headliners,
the two organisers of this concert,
please welcome Josh and Asher.'

The clapping isn't as loud
as it was for Tara but I can hear
Ruben saying, 'Yes Yes Yes'
and then the rest of the audience
join in with him.

Everyone is chanting 'Yes Yes Yes'
and Asher and I look at each other.
And we say, at exactly the same time,
'Let's rock for Ruben!'

PART 5: AT THE END OF THE DAY

When Asher and I step on stage,
everyone starts cheering.
This feels strange because
it doesn't happen in church.

When we play hymns, it's to help
the congregation to sing in time.
It's not about us, it's about Jesus.

Today, we're playing for Ruben.

When I look at him I feel like
I'm going to cry happy tears
because everyone came today
to "Rock for Ruben!" I realise
I have nothing to worry about.

I look from Ruben to Mum
and the rest of the front row,
which is full of friends from church
and friends from school.

They're ready to film our performance.
They're holding their phones up,
like they have phones for faces.

We start with everyone's favourite
"Ruben Says Yes" and, of course,
everyone joins in. It feels amazing!

Even better than our birthday!

Second, we play "Tick Tock".
Third, "At the End of the Day".

This is my favourite of Asher's songs
because it's a slow one, so it's easier
to breathe when I play along.

AT THE END OF THE DAY

At the end of the day
I count my blessings
and one of them is you

At the end of the day
I thank God
for bringing me to you

At the end of the day
I count my blessings
and one of them is you

My friend, my best friend
my friend, my best friend.

After Asher sings the words,
I have a clarinet solo
where I repeat the melody
from the beginning.
Asher joins in at the end,
singing, "My friend, my best friend."

I look at Mum and she's crying.
Aunty and Uncle are crying.

I know these are happy tears.

The audience cheer and chant
'Yes yes yes', before Ruben
even has the chance to start them off.

Now, I'm crying happy tears, too.

Then, Father Francis invites
all the performers back on stage
for another round of applause.

I wipe the tears from my eyes.

Tara stands in between
me and Asher, putting herself
centre stage. She holds
one of our hands in each of hers.

Tara raises our hands in the air,
like she's a boxing referee
and she's declared both Asher and me
as the winners.

The audience whoop and holler
even louder than before.

'You two were amazing,' says Tara,
'Maybe you could play for me?
Or maybe we can collaborate on a song
and, you know, see how it goes.'

Asher looks past Tara,
to me, and smiles.
Then, Asher says to Tara,
'You were really good too.
Josh and I will discuss it
and we'll get back to you.'

PART 6: WHAT IF

Asher and I are discussing
whether we want to collaborate with Tara,
when Mum interrupts us,
'We've counted the money from the door
and we've raised more than we need
for Ruben's new wheelchair.
So we've decided we want to use the extra
to buy you a saxophone.'

'That's amazing,' says Asher,
jumping for joy and hugging me,
which makes me jump with her.

This makes me feel excited
for a few seconds but then I think:
What if Ruben needs something else?
What if Mum needs something?
What if–
'It's okay,' I say, 'I like my clarinet.'

Asher begins: 'But Josh–'

And Ruben jumps in: 'No no no'

Have I said the wrong thing, again?

I look at Asher, then at Ruben,
and I don't know what to say.

I look at Mum for an answer.

Mum turns to Reuben:
'Don't you think Josh was amazing in the concert?
Aren't you proud of him?
And don't you think he should have a saxophone?'
And Ruben says, 'Yes yes yes'

Now I can give the clarinet back
to Father Francis, and someone else
who can't afford an instrument
can play in church band with us.

YES

WAKE

JASMINE RICHARDS
ILLUSTRATED BY WUMZUM

My Dearest Eva,

I know this is not an easy time for you. I know I am not by your side. Change is scary. It has always been so. But just as the seasons change, so must we. Just as leaves will fall, so will green shoots sprout. The box is yours now. It was given to me by my father to help prepare me for what was to come. I was only a little bit older than you when I went to the Wake for the first time. Know that I love you even if I'm not with you to hold your hand.

Yours always,

Grams

P.S Don't worry! The feathers inside this box are cruelty free. Choose the ones that speak to you. You'll know what I mean...

Eva placed the letter flat on her desk. Her fingertips then traced the cravings on the large wooden box in front of her. The indented spirals and swirls were cool and rough. Eva wondered if her grandmother had traced the same patterns with her fingertips when she had opened the box for the first time. Eva flicked the clasp and then pushed the lid back.

The inside of the box was filled with a medley of colour. Feathers of all shades lay in narrow compartments. Each segment was labelled with names and descriptions all written in her grandmother's loopy handwriting.

"Scarlett Wing. Navy-Black Longtail. Iridescent Hyacinth," Eva whispered the names into the quiet of her bedroom. "Yellow Sulphur Crested Top-Knot. Tri-colour Ombre," she continued. This time she said the names a little louder, but she hated how nervous she sounded. How her voice cracked as she read the descriptions of each of the feathers.

Eva's gaze rested on the stiff golden mask that lay at the centre of the box. Its smooth surface was a blank canvas begging to be crowned with feathers. It was still an unwritten story. Maybe if she kept on looking at its plainness, she could erase what had happened? Maybe if she kept on looking at the warmth of the gold, she could pretend that her world had not changed forever.

Eva's parents kept on telling her that everything would

be okay. They tried to reassure. To explain. But Eva wasn't ready to hear it. She just wanted to be alone.

She chewed on the end of one of her long braids. The habit drove her mum crazy, but Grams was always quick to say, "Leave the child be, Lyssa. What harm is she doing?"

"What harm," Eva said out loud. I can do plenty of harm. Eva knew that now. For a moment an image of the scorch marks she had seared across the playing field filled her head.

Eva screwed her eyes shut. They still felt gritty and warm and she remembered how her gaze had become blazing hot. How the rays had flared out of her eyes and ripped through the air.

She wished Grams was here. Eva didn't know how she was supposed to handle any of this. She was a freak of nature with fire in her eyes. Then, there was the looming shadow of what was going to happen that afternoon at the Wake. The speeches. The solemn faces. All those people dressed in black.

Taking a breath, Eva opened her eyes and stared at the box again. Focus on the feathers, she told herself. Choose some. That is what her grandmother had instructed. Rainbow Hybrid. Camelot Golden Rust. Shamrock Green. Grams' letter said that the feathers would talk to her. That they would tell her which ones to choose.

Eva picked up the feather titled Camelot Golden Rust.

Its yellow edges were soft against her palm but there was only silence in her head. She picked up a Rainbow Hybrid feather next. Nothing. Still nothing. Grams had lied to her. It wasn't the first time. Her whole family had lied to her. Except for Marvin. She needed to remember that they had lied to her brother too.

Eva glanced at the framed photo on her desk. Grams had her arms wrapped around her. They were at Carnival. Grams' mask was covered in jewels and its red feathers curled like flames around her face and head. People danced all around them but in the middle of the storm of bodies, Eva and Grams were still. They were both smiling. So hard. Eva's cheeks ached even looking at the photo. And through the mask, Eva could see the love shining out of her grandmother's eyes.

Eva reached for another feather. According to the label, it was a Navy-Black Longtail. This feather was almost as long as her forearm. She held it by its sharp tip and traced a symbol softly on the desk. She felt the whisper of the words 'happy here with you' touch her mind.

Thud, thud, thud. The loud knocking at her bedroom door made Eva jump. It couldn't be time yet could it? She looked at the clock – it was still only 10am. The Wake wasn't until 2.

It's the police. The thought invaded her mind. She

felt her insides twist like the tangle of weeds in their garden. The same weeds that Mum accused Dad of never dealing with.

They've come to arrest me. Eva trembled. They know about my powers.

THUD, THUD, THUD.

The knocking on the door was louder this time and more impatient. No, not the police. Maybe it's the scientists, her thoughts said. The feather said nothing in return and so she put it down. Yep, it'll be a whole bunch of people in white coats with clipboards and test tubes and petri dishes and microsc–

The door crashed open and Marvin stood in the doorway. His eyes looked red. Like he'd been crying. No way, Eva thought. Her big brother never cried. Not even when his team got relegated to the Championship.

"Didn't you hear me knocking?" Marvin demanded.

"I thought you had a petri dish," Eva explained.

Marvin kissed his teeth ,and it was like he was sucking all the air out of the room and through his pursed lips. "You're making zcro sense." He shook his head. "Maybe that's the way it's gonna be from now on." He jerked his head over to the stairs. "Alyssa and Leroy want to talk to you. They're in the kitchen."

"I don't want to speak to Mum and Dad."

"Well, you need to. Time's running out." Marvin's shoulders hunched. "It'll be The Wake soon."

"I don't want to go." Eva could hear the pleading in her voice.

Marvin laughed bitterly. "We're way past that now, sis."

"Why does it have to be like this," Eva whispered.

"I don't know, but it is what it is." Marvin strode away.

Stepping into the hallway, Eva peered over the edge of the banister. Light spilled out from the kitchen and she could hear the familiar tones of Mum and Dad. They were arguing. She could hear snatches of words. Powers. Eva. Danger. Eva. The Wake. Eva. Today. Eva.

She swallowed hard before hopping onto the bannister and sliding down to the bottom. Funny. She hadn't done that for years, but in a few hours nothing was ever going to be the same again. Why not let herself remember the kid she used to be?

Mum and Dad were sitting at the kitchen table. They both looked tense and jumped up as soon as she entered the room. The room smelt of spices and thyme and Eva realised that Dad must be cooking brown stew chicken. They were going to need to eat after the Wake after all.

"Eva." Mum didn't seem to know what to do with her hands. They fluttered about like a trapped butterfly.

"Eviekins." Dad stood.

Eva shook her head. "Don't call me that, Dad. I'm not a baby anymore. I don't even know what I am."

Mum's shoulders stiffened. "You're our daughter. Nothing's changed."

Eva crossed her arms. "How can you say that? Everything's changed and you know it."

"We should have told you earlier." A nerve twitched along Dad's jaw as he sat once more. "We should have told you and Marvin. That way you would have been prepared."

"Seriously?" Mum's hands splayed flat on the table. "That's how we're going to play this? Regret changes nothing. We did things the way you wanted. The way your mother wanted."

"I know, Lyssa." Dad rubbed at his forehead. "But Mum isn't here and we are. We've got to fix this. Help Eva understand."

Fix this. Fix me. "I'm sorry." The word burst out of Eva's mouth. "I'm sorry that I'm like this. I'm sorry that we even have to go to the Wake."

"Honey," Mum said, rushing over to her. "It's going to be okay."

Dad slumped down further into a kitchen chair. "Maybe it is too soon," Eva thought she heard him murmur.

Mum took Eva's face in her hands. "It's time for us to talk about this properly. Tell me how it felt when the fire came." Her voice was gentle.

So, Eva did. She told her parents how she saw Afua being

picked on by some kids from the year above. How they'd emptied all the stuff out of her bag and were chucking her favourite novel around like a Frisbee on the Green. Eva told them how her eyes felt hot and then how light blasted from them. She told them how the bullies ran off. How Afua ran off – looking at her like she was a stranger.

As she finished, Mum took her Eva's hands into her grasp.

"Why do you think the fire came?" Mum asked.

"I was angry," Eva muttered. "Afua was upset."

"So, you were trying to help," Mum said.

"Yeah, I guess," Eva replied. "But what if those kids say something? I've seen enough films to know what happens next." Images of scientists and police floated into her mind once more.

Eva's mum laughed softly. "Don't worry about that," she said. "It's all been dealt with."

"Dealt with?" Eva repeated.

"There's ways to undo what has been seen," Mum explained. "You've just got to ask the right person."

"Is that why Afua's not texted me?" Eva asked.

Mum nodded. "She doesn't remember any of it now and that's for the best. We've got to keep your powers secret." She kissed Eva's hands. "You'll be one of the youngest Manifesters on record, that's for sure." Mum almost sounded proud.

Eva snatched her hand away. “I don’t want to be the youngest anything.”

“It’s your heritage.” Mum’s voice was soothing. “It’s who you were born to be. Just like your grandmother.”

Eva stared at her mother. She still looked like Mum. Long goddess locs. Black glasses. A dark grey dress. Yet the words coming out of her mouth were strange. And so certain.

Eva remembered the game she would play with Grams. They would invent stories for people they saw in the park or at the supermarket. Give them superhero powers. Aliases. Grams said that all humans were mysteries. That all humans had secrets. Eva hadn’t known she’d been talking about herself. Or Mum. Or Dad.

Mum guided Eva to a chair and sat her down.

“I’m sorry we didn’t tell you earlier,” Mum said. “Your grandmother said it would be better to let you and Marvin just be kids. After all, we didn’t even know if you guys would manifest.”

“I never did,” Dad said, still slumped in his chair. “I hoped the same might be true for you and your brother.”

Mum stood behind Dad and put a hand on his shoulder. “Before I married your dad I didn’t know any of this super power stuff even existed.” She shook her head. “It was quite a surprise when I found out what my mother-in-law and others like her could do." She squeezed Dad's shoulder. "Go on, show her. She deserves the whole truth."

Dad took a tiny black device that Eva had never seen from his pocket. A beam of light arced into the room and a hologram flickered into life.

It took a moment for Eva to realize it, but the projection was of her grandmother. But she looked different. Real different.

Grams was dressed in a black suit that was imprinted with stars that seemed to be made up of pulsing threads of power. She wore a mask that looked very similar to the one she always had at Carnival. But there was a big difference. The red feathers on this mask were actual flames. And they curled around her face in fiery tendrils.

"Meet Blaze," Mum said. "Your grandmother's superhero alias."

"My mum," Dad said. He looked proud.

Eva could not take her eyes off the hologram who was currently demonstrating a series of complicated kung-fu moves at a ridiculous speed whilst occasionally shooting golden rays from her eyes. Her grandmother looked... awesome. Strong. Fast. Beautiful.

"I wish she was here," Eva said.

"Me too," came Marvin's voice.

Eva turned to see her brother in the doorway.

Dad leapt from his chair and wrapped Marvin in an embrace. "I'm glad you changed your mind and decided to come and join us. This is your story too."

"But I can't do what Eva can," Marvin muttered. "It's not fair."

"You can't do it right now," Dad said. "Your powers might come later." He sat Marvin next to Eva. "Or, they might not come at all but you can still help."

"How?" Marvin asked.

"Well, fighting crime and defending the universe is actually a bit of a family business," Dad explained. "Me and your mum help out even though we don't have powers." Dad smiled encouragingly. "We do the admin. Diary planning. Not an easy task when superheroes live all over the world."

"All of them undercover," Mum added.

Marvin rolled his eyes. "So Eva gets to shoot death rays from her eyes and I'll get a crash course in spreadsheets."

"Marvin, it's not like that," Mum said. "Oh, I wish your grandmother was here to explain."

"But she's not," Dad said. "So I'll tell you what she would tell you. Be proud of the contribution you make. That's what's in your power."

Eva's throat felt tight, wishing Grams was the one saying these words.

"Listen you two, protecting this planet is something we've been doing for generations." Dad began tapping at the device again and Grams was replaced by an image of a boy with skin the colour of rain-soaked earth. He was wrapped in a cloak of azure blue and held a staff covered in carvings up to the sky.

"This is Ewedo," Dad explained. "He was the son of a great astronomer who lived many hundreds of years ago in the Ancient City of Benin. His father studied the sun, the stars and the moon to help his people tell the seasons or identify when important ceremonies should take place. His knowledge of the sky was passed down from generation to generation."

Eva stared at Ewedo. He was not much older than her. But somehow the boy in blue looked so much wiser. From the curve of his cheek to the way his hands clasped the staff so confidently.

"But with Ewedo it was different," Dad went on. "He wasn't just an observer of the stars. The stars lived within him. They gave him ancient knowledge. They gave him the speed of light. They gave him power."

Mum smiled. "In your father's family, that power has been passed on from parent to child or grandparent to grandchild for centuries now. That's why you can shoot light from eyes, Eva. Who knows what else you might be able to do? That's what we need to find out."

"I didn't know we came from an ancient kingdom in Africa," Eva breathed. "I thought our family came from the Caribbean?"

"Our family's history is long and winding," Dad said. "And it is a blend of many places and cultures." He looked serious. "There was a time in history when our powers were not there to help us."

"But seasons change," Eva said, repeating the words in Gram's letter. "Just as leaves will fall, so will green shoots sprout."

Dad nodded; his eyes proud. "Exactly." He put the device down and the boy disappeared. "Eviekins, these powers don't define you. They don't change you."

Marvin scrunched up his face. "Um, they kind of do, Dad." He shrugged. "She'll need to learn what it means to be a superhero. How to harness her powers." He looked off into the distance. "It's definitely going to need a montage."

Eva crossed her arms. "Marvin this is my life! Not a movie!"

Mum smiled. "I think you guys watch too much TV. Come, let's get ready for the Wake."

*

Eva did not want to get out of the car, and she felt her chest tighten as Mum switched off the engine. They had parked in front of a tall stone building. It had no windows, but the towering doors were wide open and cloaked figures were streaming in.

Eva spotted a couple of people she recognised through the car's window. Miss Ida and Gladys. She always called them aunty even though they were very distant relatives. They would often be round at Grams' house when Eva visited after school. They looked very serious now as they entered the building to attend the Wake. Eva took a deep breath.

"Ready." Mum had turned in her seat and was looking over her shoulder at Eva and Marvin.

Marvin squeezed Eva's hand. "Don't worry, Sis. We'll do this together."

Eva swallowed and nodded. She opened the car door and stepped out onto the pavement. The air was warm. Eva felt stifling hot wrapped up in her long cloak, but her parents said she must keep it on. At least until they entered the building.

Eva could feel the gaze of interest on her as people walked past but she refused to make eye contact. She looked down at her shoes noticing the thick mud that was streaked across the shiny patent leather. The sight of her mucky shoes made her want to laugh somehow. Imagine coming to the Wake with unpolished shoes. Grams would have laughed as well at that. If she was here with me.

Eva scrubbed at her face. The shoes had been on the to-do list but finishing the mask had taken a lot longer than any of them had expected. Eva hands had trembled terribly whenever she tried to add a feather to the mask. In the end, Marvin, Mum and Dad had all helped.

Eva would touch a feather and work out if it was speaking to her and then Marvin would fire up the glue-gun. Dad would cut down the spines of the feathers if they were too long and Mum would hold the feather in place until the glue hardened. Then they used thin threads of wire to make sure the feathers were really secure.

"Why are we even doing this?" Marvin had asked, as he's scooped up yet another glue stick and eyed up one of the navy-black feathers.

"It's needed for the Wake," Dad had said. "You'll understand when we get there."

Dad had now got out of the car. The mask had been lying on his lap for the whole of the journey, but he now carefully handed it to Eva.

"You got it?" he asked.

"I've got it," Eva said.

It really is beautiful, Eva thought, as the mask shimmered in the sunlight. They'd left the gold of the mask completely plain, but the feathers were ridiculously flamboyant and stretched upwards in a skyscraper of colour. The navy-blue feathers were the most common plumes but here and there was a red feather or a yellow one or a green. The feathers wove in and out of each other so intricately it felt like you were looking into a kaleidoscope.

Eva had a sudden urge to throw the mask on the ground and stamp on it. As if that will change anything, she thought. We'd still have to go into the Wake. Nothing was going to change that.

Her mum linked an arm through hers and then they were walking. They climbed the steps that led to the building's entrance. A tall man, with deep brown skin stretched over high cheekbones stood at the top. He gave Eva a smile so wide and so warm that it made Eva stumble for a moment. She hadn't been expecting that.

"Don't look so sad, Eva," the man said. "You look like you're about to go to a funeral."

Eva bit her lip. Embarrassed.

"She's just a bit nervous, Gideon," Dad said. "The Wake will be her first one. I'm sure you remember yours."

Gideon nodded. "I most certainly do." He dipped his head. "It was magic. You'll see."

Eva stepped into the building. She was in a room with a vaulted roof and it was cool in here. There was music. The steady beat of a drum filled her head. All around her, the gathered had taken off their cloaks to reveal black costumes adorned with stars. They were all wearing their masks edged with feathers, but their faces were not solemn. Every single superhero was smiling. As Eva looked at each one more closely, she could see that the feathers on their masks were transforming into fire, or water, or twisting vines or plumes of mist.

Mum gently unlinked their arms. "You've got this Eva. Just walk to the front." She took Eva's cloak revealing the superhero uniform beneath it.

Dad kissed Eva's forehead and Marvin gave her a little push. "See you on the other side, Sis."

Eva walked forwards clutching her mask. Everyone around her was whooping and clapping. Some were even dancing. Each step felt like she was walking closer to the edge of a towering cliff but the cheers around her carried her onwards.

And then, she materialized. Grams. Eva's grandmother was standing there. Dressed as Blaze, with her mask edged with fire. Grams.

Her grandmother held her arms wide open and Eva ran into them. And then they were hugging as tight as anything.

The mask crushed between them.

"Grams, I missed you," Eva said.

"I missed you too, Eva," Grams whispered. "I wanted to see you, but I had to get this all organized." She pulled back and looked down at her. "What a terror you are, manifesting like that, and so young as well."

Eva shrugged. "I didn't mean to, it just kind of happened."

"I heard," Grams said. "The thing is, as soon as powers manifest the Wake must happen as soon as possible, so the awakened powers can be honoured."

"I know, Mum and Dad tried to tell me yesterday but I wasn't really ready to hear it," Eva confessed.

"Forgive me for not being with you. I know the last 24 hours have not been easy," Grams kissed her forehead. "Now we must help your powers settle into the right pattern." She took the mask from Eva's hands and looked at it. "Goodness child look what you've made here. Something very special indeed."

Well, I had lots of help, Eva thought to herself.

Grams turned Eva to face the crowd and the gathered fell silent. Blaze held up the mask.

"Eva has chosen her feathers and in turn her powers have chosen her. Her mask tells us that she is something extraordinary. We have fire here. We have air. We have earth and water too. Who knows what powers Eva will manifest?"

There were gasps around the room and low murmurings of surprise.

Eva spotted her brother watching from the shadows. Mum and Dad were standing with him. All their faces were filled with pride. Pride and love.

This is it, Eva thought. Grams was about to put the mask on her for the first time. Eva would learn what her powers were. All of them. She'd be a proper superhero after this.

"Grams, stop!" Eva's voice echoed around the room.

Grams' eyes widened in shock and worry. "Eva, what is it?"

"I can't do this.

Not without my family," she explained. "I made this mask with them. "They need to be up here as well."

Grams' smile was wide and Eva could see the love shining in her eyes even through the mask. "Then you'd better call them up here."

Eva beckoned her mum, dad and Marvin over. They came to stand by her side.

She turned to face her grandmother. She looked at the mask and tilted her face upwards. "I'm ready."

1:43

TOMORROW, AS IN

YOMI ṢODE

ILLUSTRATED BY WILLKAY

Today, Dad kisses me on the cheek then signals for me to meet him at the bus stop, like normal, as I've always done. But today was different. Today, there's a beat in my step, tiny kicks & snares - boots & cats'n through my body, dribbling between organs & finally jump shooting out of my mouth, *Dad, meet me half way! Not the bus stop, ok?, I'll call you. Love youuu!!*

Scoring my grown point! Turning then bopping away as he eyes every trail, following the ooze of swag I left behind until he shouts, *Hey! Badman. Whoever she is, just make sure your nerves don't make you fart, innit. Love youuuuuu!*

Though I know Dad's joking, I can't unhear the possibilities of my flatulence & the orchestral sound of laughter coming from my bredrins, What if it bubbles in my stomach in my excitement? Nah! What if the smell lingers like Dad's *Don't fart innit!* Haunting me like some ghost! Naah! No *waaay!* I repeat to myself.

Now my *No waaaay* can't be unthought. Can't be unseen, unimagined, Fam - this morning, my nerves were unstuck! The beat in my step was King T'challa, it was Stormzy, it was all Black & excellent & before Dad interrupted & started talking about farts - it was her. It was homework club with her & thinking about the walk to the bus stop, feeling as though my powers stopped time when she said, *I can take that route home as well! So, tomorrow, yeah?* Her.

Today. As in *tomorrow* is today & until I arrived at school, everything was twice! I brushed my teeth twice, I sprayed deodorant in each armpit twice and today is a feeling I cannot explain. It's an elbow nudge to my rib for saying something silly, then faking the pain like it really hurt. It's transparency to the girl I'm feeling that my Dad joked I'd fart, out of nerves. It's the girl I'm feeling laughing & asking if my farts smell. It's me being grossed out that she's entertaining fart talk & knowing this was never about farts. It's the slowest walk to the bus stop, not holding hands but wanting to. It's the ride halfway, the *see you tomorrow?* The *No!* when Dad asks if I have a crush on her & the *Yes please*, in the morning, when Dad says with a smile, *The same plan as yesterday?*

THE AFTER EVER AFTER BUREAU

PATRICE LAWRENCE

ILLUSTRATED BY ONYINYE IWU

Excellent walk with guide, Cindi. Her gossip about the British royal family and their gruesome history with the Tower of London was especially satisfying.

M Markle, California

Marla unhooked her skin from the back of the door and slipped it back on. That moment when she changed from speeding ball of fire to human girl was always a strange one. She felt cold and heavy and her legs and arms were just TOO SLOW. In some ways it should be easier for Mum. She'd been doing this transformation thing since she was a kid. But it still took longer for Mum to repellisate. Marla frowned to herself. Was that even a real word? It was definitely the word Mum used for putting her skin back on when she eventually found it. But she could never remember where she left it. Soucouyants were much misunderstood. Mum says it was sexism. Marla thought it was more likely to do with the fact that they were flying shape-shifters with the habit of sucking people's blood. (Modern super-strength iron pills had rendered that part of soucouyanting redundant now.) But what it did mean, was that if a woman was suspected of being a soucouyant in the old times, some idiot would wait until she was on a night flight then set out to find her skin. And rub salt on it so she couldn't get back in. So Mum was taught to hide her skin very carefully. It also explained why Mum only ever had vinegar on her chips.

'Have you checked the laundry basket?' Marla called.

'Good idea,' Mum called back.

Mum came out of the bedroom and into the hallway. She looked like Mum, but just paler. And more glowy. And more see-through. She went into the bathroom.

'Good call! It's in here!' She came back out holding an Aldi bag. 'Get some sleep in, now, Marla. We've got a whole heap of work for later.'

Marla climbed into her bed. She always kept her curtains open so she could see dawn breaking over Peckham. There was six weeks of holiday before she started Year 7 at Peckham Beckham Academy. She had envied some of the other kids in her class who were going off on big adventures with their families, swimming with turtles in Tobago or climbing mountains in Scotland, before the leap into secondary school. She would be staying right here in Peckham, but every night her and mum would soar over London and beyond, seeing the world in a way that classmates never could. Last night, they had followed the spots of light south along the motorways to the coast and watched the dark hulks of boats cross the sea under the bright smudge of the Milky Way. As the rising sun turned the windows in the block opposite pink and orange, she fell asleep.

Marla woke up – well, Mum was claiming it was six hours later, but it felt like six minutes. But, Marla knew there was work to do. August was the busiest time for the After Ever After Bureau and she and Mum had to make sure everything was ready.

What is the After Ever After Bureau? Well, a 'bureau' can be two things. It can be an agency that delivers particular services or it can be a writing desk with many drawers. The After Ever After Bureau most certainly does offer a very particular service. And a writing desk? It's for... well... writing. It can be used for writing letters, or diaries or stories. Think about the stories.

Imagine every drawer holds a different story full of different characters. When the story as you know it has ended, the drawer isn't pushed shut. There will always be more story left; the characters live on. They push open their story drawers, climb out and look around.

The After Ever After Bureau offers its particular service to fatigued fairytale folk who want to have normal human experiences, mythical beings who want to disappear for a few weeks, legends who feel that they have the sky on their shoulders and need some downtime. Marla and her Mum connect the jaded folk from fairytales, myths and legends with unique and unparalleled experiences in the real world. Last year, Sleeping Beauty shadowed the director of the Jo Whisk Exercise Corp, learning new ways to combat a sluggish metabolism and the urge to take day-long siestas. Newly-divorced Cinderella led very successful guided tours around the Tower of London. You get the picture. Although there is a call for this service all year round, summer and Christmas are the busiest times. For some reason, the FML (that's fairytale, myth and legend) folk actually enjoy crowds. Perhaps it's because so many of them spent the early years of their stories lonely and mostly friendless.

The plan was to start the day with brunch. Marla was

always ravenous after a flight, but Mum said it was bad to sleep on a full stomach.

'Fancy the Hotch Pot?' Mum asked.

Of course! Banana pancakes with blueberries. Saltfish fritters and fried plantain. Egg and beans. All on one enormous plate. Yet again, they had to take the stairs in their block instead of the lift. Six flights going down wasn't bad. It was the way back that Marla dreaded.

The strangeness started after brunch. Mum had forgotten her scarf on the back of the chair and ran back to get it. Marla was standing by the electrical shop on the corner considering if Mum would notice if she had a little bit of a nap before she started work. The shop always displayed a massive TV in the window. It was tuned into a kids channel. A man dressed in a bright green boiler suit had a book open on his lap. A crowd of young kids sat on a carpet in front of him. He grinned and held up the book for the camera. Marla smiled. It was a version of Cinderella and the illustration showed the princess marrying her Prince Charming. The camera then panned to show the audience's happy faces.

The storyteller turned another page. Right. Maybe this version gave a happy ending to the stepmother and her daughters too. Except the storyteller wasn't grinning anymore. He looked confused. The camera operator must have been gesturing to him because he held the book up again, page open. The picture was of Cinderella and Prince Charming each sitting on the far end of a sofa, crying their eyes out. What? That's not right! The fairytales are only supposed to show up to the happy endings, not what happens afterwards.

The words underneath said: And soon afterwards they realised they didn't like each other and went their separate ways.

The letters seemed to fly off the page, twirl in the air and then stick to the camera because they filled the whole, gigantic screen.

Then it cut to a cartoon.

Marla was so busy thinking about the weird ending, she didn't notice the six flights of stairs back to their flat.

Marla and Mum settled down at the table they used for work, laptops back-to-back. Each time they logged on, they ran a virus scan; they didn't want all their clients real identities leaked to the world. The virus scan started. Then it stopped. Then it started again. Mum and Marla looked at each other over their laptops.

'We just had a synchronised glitch, right?' Mum asked.

Marla nodded. She supposed the glitches could happen at

the same time if they were both running exactly the same programme at exactly the same time on exactly the same hardware. The laptop was running all right now, though.

Mum said, 'I've sent you a list of clients coming over in the first two weeks of August. Got the Frog Princess and her little brother, Tad. And Puss In Boots. It's a quick stay as he's heading to New Zealand for a soul weekend in Wellington. Then there's that girl with the jar. I can't remember her name. Can you check for any potential disasters?'

Marla nodded. She clicked on the first file. Tad Royale, the Frog Princess's youngest son. He was more froggier than his other siblings. He wanted to spend a few months in Ecuador learning how to fly after seeing some gliding leaf frogs on a nature programme. Mum's note was to check how long he could hold his frog shape. They didn't want him gliding off a tree as a frog and becoming man-shaped halfway down.

Marla's screen when blank.

'What the…?' Mum said.

They both looked at their screens then each other. A little red box flashed in the middle of the screen.

You have 1 notification.

'Okay,' Mum said, slowly. 'All this just to let us know that we've had a review?'

You have 12 notifications.

'Um...' Marla said.

'Oh,' Mum said.

You have 43 notifications.

'Forty-three reviews,' Marla said. 'All in one go. Maybe they were jammed in the system?'

'I suppose we better see what they say,' Mum said.

'I don't think we need to,' Marla said, quietly.

The notification box had disappeared. Letters whirled around the screen, just as they had on the big TV in the electric shop. An alarm went off. Not the alarm that Marla had set to wake her up on school mornings. No, this noise was so loud Marla was surprised that the rest of the block's residents hadn't thrown open their windows to check that a spaceship hadn't landed nearby.

'Marla!' Mum yelled. 'How do we stop it?'

'I don't know how!'

Suddenly, there was silence, though Marla's ears were still ringing. The letters stopped whirling. The colours blasted from the screen, bright orange on black.

HAPPY EVER AFTER IS FAKE NEWS! ALL PATHS LEAD TO MISERY!

The computer turned itself off and stayed that way.

Mum stood up shakily. 'We've been compromised,' she said.

Marla pushed the 'on/off' button again. There was nothing apart from the reflection of her face in the dark screen. 'What does that mean?'

'It means that a villain on The Other Side wants to make our world believe that there is no happily ever after.'

'Who would do such a thing?'

Mum laughed. It was a shocked laugh.

'There's a few miserable characters who've probably been thinking about this for years,' Mum said. 'The Wicked Stepmother has always had a grudge.'

'So you think it could be her?'

'No! This is too...' She tapped her screen. 'Too sophisticated. Not her style. She'd take out an advert saying 'Cinderella smells' and paste it to every shoe shop window.'

'So who, then?'

'I don't know.' Mum pushed herself away from the table. 'But I know a woman who would be good at finding out.'

Marla's mouth fell open. 'You don't mean...'

Mum nodded firmly. 'It's time to bring Grandma out of retirement for one last job.'

Grandma Suki had been minding her own business when the call came. She had done twenty years at the Bureau and had been happy to hand it over to her daughter, Alvi, and her granddaughter, Marla. They were entirely capable. She had retired back to Trinidad and built a nice house not far from the Caroni swamp. She'd sit there in the evenings watching the scarlet ibis flock to their roost at sunset and playing 'snap' with Papa Bois and Mama D'Leau. She was even the patron of the local jumbie jamboree. And she was –

BORED!

Her brain was turning to guava jelly. There must be more to enjoying life as your local neighbourhood soucouyant than this? It seemed not. Until Alvi called. Grandma said 'goodbye' to her friends, locked up her house and asked a loup garou to keep an eye on things. There's nothing like a headless muscleman wrapped in chains to ward off casual onlookers. As soon as sunset fell, she packed her skin into her favourite holdall and blazed off into the sky. Ten hours later, she was in Peckham.

It had felt like a long time since Marla had seen Grandma Suki. Mum said it was only five years, but five years ago, Marla had actually been five. How different she was then! Marla had always known that she was a soucouyant from a long line of proud soucouyants. She'd also always known about the After Ever After Bureau.

But to have Grandma back again made her want to soar through the sky right now

Grandma looked like she was buzzing with energy. She'd slept for a couple of hours, taken a shower and eaten a hefty breakfast. She looked comfortable in her skin. It was probably down to the amount of cocoa butter she used. Marla had to focus now. They had a job to do.

Grandma had asked Mum for an update and was scribbling notes on her tablet.

'So what did they have to say?' Grandma asked.

Mum sighed. 'The werewolves of London?'

Grandma nodded.

'Awoooo.'

Grandma rolled her eyes. 'Still making no sense. I suppose it's a full moon in two nights. Their big furry heads can't think of anything else. Any other leads?'

'I had a quick ask around the all-night bowling alley,' Mum said. 'I managed to have a word with Sysiphus. He laughed and said that anyone who reads Greek myths knows that nothing ever ends happily for anyone. They don't have to pretend to live happily ever after. He reckons it's nothing to do with the myths, so it must be the fairytale or legend sides.'

'Yes,' Grandma said. 'That figures.'

'But there was something strange,' Mum said. 'Sysiphus was losing the game.'

'Losing the game?' Marla and Grandma said it at the same time, then grinned at each other.

'Gosh,' Mum said. 'You two have exactly the same smile!'

'How could he lose?' Marla asked.

Sisyphus was a legendary cheat. He'd even cheated Death twice.

'Exactly,' Mum said. 'But I did catch the name of the person he was losing to. It was on the screen above their lane. Peter Parker.'

Marla frowned. 'Peter Parker? Like in Spiderman?'

Grandma flicked her a side eye. 'Yes, Marla. Spiderman. But I believe that we may be dealing with the original, Lord Anansi.'

'Ah,' Mum said. 'So THAT's where the hacker found their web expertise.'

'So what are we waiting for?' Marla stood up. 'Let's go find him, then.'

Mum stayed seated. 'I suppose we'll have to wait for tonight. Sisyphus will definitely be after a rematch. He can't stand losing.'

'True.' Grandma stood up too. 'But I have a very good idea where Anansi will be now.'

The British Library is a large redbrick building set back from one of the busiest roads in London. Marla, Mum and Grandma walked through the gates into the courtyard. Marla had forgotten that the reason why Anansi was such a good trickster was because he was always looking for more knowledge. He wanted to own all the wisdom and all the stories.

'I think he'll be in the Kings Library section,' Mum said. 'How could he resist all those shiny shelves of old books?'

'I'm not sure,' Grandma said. 'There's knowledge in secrets too. I think he would have taken his spider-self down into the underground stacks. Aren't there miles upon miles of books down there? He wants the knowledge that no one else thinks is important.'

'Um…. Mum? Grandma?' Marla was staring at the statue in the courtyard. It was an enormous, seated man bent double as he measured the ground with a pair of compasses. Something wasn't quite right.

'It's Isaac Newton,' Mum said. 'The scientist.'

'Yes,' Grandma said. 'And if he asks no questions, he will hear no flies.'

'Sorry, Mama?' Mum looked concerned. 'Are you sure you rested long enough after your flight?'

Grandma pointed to the webs on the statue. 'See what our clever little Marla spotted?'

Marla glowed with happiness (but not too much; this

wasn't the right time to turn into a ball of fire).

'He will hear no flies because they will be caught in a web long before they reach. Come on, Lord Anansi!' Grandma called. 'Show yourself.'

A few seconds later, a spider scurried out of the statue's ear. It swung from a fine thread onto the statue's wrist, then slid down the compass on to the ground. And then, it was a man. He was completely bald but with a strip of short grey beard down the centre of his chin. His eyes were large and dark grey. He seemed to be looking at you and all around you at the same time. He was wearing a baggy grey velvet suit and a pale pink shirt. Rather than a tie, he wore a sliver of white ribbon in a narrow bow beneath his chin. The pointed corners of the ends reminded Marla of fangs. She wondered if the long loose jacket was to hide the other four limbs or if the other legs just disappeared when he changed.

'Ladies!' He bowed deeply.

Grandma stepped towards him. He stepped back. 'Don't 'Lady' me,' she said. 'What are you doing here?'

'Enjoying the view, Madam Suki. I actually feel quite insulted that you think I would hole up inside when there are so many rich stories to be heard, so many new things to learn, just by being still and silent.' He smiled at them all.

'And, of course, it helps if you're inside a giant ear.'

Grandma stepped forward again. Anansi stepped back. A few more centimetres and he would be sitting on Sir Isaac's lap. 'What new thing have you learned, Lord Anansi?'

'The number 73 bus no longer terminates at Victoria.'

This time it was Grandma's turn to glow. Smoked wisped up from the ankles of her jeggings and a tiny crease of flame smouldered below her chin.

'Okay, Madam Suki!' Anansi fanned himself. 'No need to get hot under the collar! What can I do for you?'

'Someone is trying to sabotage happiness. What's going on?'

'That's a big question, Madam Suki. Narrow your search and try again.' Anansi clapped his hand to his mouth.

There was silence.

'Narrow your search and try again? So that web development course we organised for you was useful then,' Grandma said coolly.

'Might have been...'

Mum moved towards Anansi. Marla was surprised to see that Mum looked sparky too. Mum had taught her that they should always be fully human in the day time, especially in public.

'You hear me, Lord A?' Grandma said. 'We are not in the mood for any of your tricks today.'

'Tell us now!' Mum's voice virtually rumbled. 'Did you hack

our systems?'

Anansi held up his hands. His palms were covered in light grey fur. 'Yes! It was me! But only that! Nothing else!'

'You hacked us and shut us down! Only that!' Mum took out her phone. She clicked on a review site and turned it to show him.

FAKE NEWS! THERE IS NO HAPPY EVER AFTER!

'What's this about then?' Mum said sternly.

Anansi looked her in the eye. Actually, he looked all three of them in the eye at the same time. Marla wished she wasn't so impressed by him.

'I really don't know who's at the centre of it. I had a Whatsapp from my old IT tutor. He said some friends wanted to test their firewall so could I hack in to pretend to bring it down. They gave me the data, I wrote some code and passed it back. And that's it!'

'And you just happen to be here when all this is kicking off?' Mum said.

'I'm on holiday!' He leaned towards Grandma. 'I know I should have a quiet life, but sometimes I just long for the hum of the city. Do you know what I mean?'

Grandma breathed in deeply. Then out. 'Who's bringing the misery, Anansi?'

'I don't know. And I don't know about 'bringing'. It's already here.'

Suddenly, the man was gone. And the crying began. A long, forlorn wailing from the bottom of an anguished heart, so deep it could have been coming from the book stacks. They looked around. Over by the café, a man was trying to comfort a little girl who was clutching a book by her side.

'But the wolf can't eat her,' she sobbed.

'There should be more!' The man held up the book. 'The story shouldn't end there!'

And she wasn't alone. A woman was sitting on the bench staring at an i-pad. She showed it to her friend sitting next to her. There were tears pouring down their cheeks.

'You… you… said this one had a happy ending!'

'Let's regroup back at the flat,' Grandma said.

Marla, Mum and Grandma trudged up the six flights of stairs. Well, Mum and Marla did. Grandma said that there was no way she was dealing with that type of nonsense. She zipped behind the recycling bins, popped out of her skin and gave it to Mum to bring up for her. Then she fired up and soared towards the sixth floor.

'I hope she realises that we haven't left a window open,' Mum said.

Grandma was less than happy when Marla and Mum arrived. She'd had to turn down her fire to a mere glow to avoid the attention of Peckham Fire Station. However, that put her on the radar of every magpie in south London.

'They're beaky blighters, that lot,' she complained. 'No manners at all.'

They sat around the table making a list of everything they knew so far. They kept the television on, but muted, so they could keep an eye on the misery. Right now, a skinny guy in checked trousers was being interviewed about how he was never taken seriously after he lured away the rats and children. He looks intently at the camera. The caption scrolls below him:

There is no happy ever after. It's all fake news.

'The Pied Piper,' Mum says. 'He's being doing the chat circuit for years. It looks like he's finally being taken seriously.'

'Who would have a grudge against us?' Marla's pencil was poised over her notepad.

'Well,' Mum said. 'Sisyphus was right about the myths. No one comes out of them well. That lot don't need to prove anything.'

'So let's think legends,' Grandma said.

'Robin Hood?' Mum asked. 'Didn't he say his life didn't have any purpose anymore. Didn't we organise something for him?'

Marla nodded. 'We got him a few sessions as one of those door-to-door charity collectors. He said he'd rather fight Little John and the Sheriff of Nottingham while blindfolded in a pit full of cold custard than do that again.'

'He was unhappy then?' Grandma asked.

'No!' Mum looked outraged at the suggestion. 'He was very happy with our service. He said it helped him value what he had.'

'So we can cross him off our list,' Grandma said, looking at Marla.

Marla was going to say that he wasn't on the list in the first place but wrote down 'Robin Hood' and put a cross through it. It would be best to keep Grandma happy. On they went, trying to remember all the fairytale folk who'd been through the Bureau. Luckily, Grandma had kept paper files in the early days, so the older ones were easier to find. Marla and Mum had to really strain their brains to remember whose unique and unparalleled experiences were buried in their computer hard drive.

Marla looked down at pages and pages of notes. This wasn't helping. There were characters from virtually every fairytale she knew, and many that she didn't.

She said, 'Maybe we do need to do what Lord Anansi said.'

Mum nodded. 'Narrow the search.'

Marla tapped her pencil on the table. She realised that Grandma and Mum were doing exactly the same thing. 'What do we need to find out?'

'Why do this now?' Mum said.

Marla opened a fresh page in her notebook and scribbled it down.

'And what do they really want?' Grandma added. 'Humans are used to misery, but they also have such short attention spans. They'll just write more happy stories and him...' She nodded towards the Pied Piper, 'he'll have his five minutes of fame barbecuing rats on I'm A Celebrity then go sloping back to the Other Side. Keeping this world miserable all the time takes effort.'

'Other motives?' Mum asked.

Marla thought hard. 'To stress us out?'

'Yes,' Grandma encouraged. 'We're getting somewhere. If the Bureau came under stress, what would you do?'

Mum and Marla looked at Grandma.

'Call you!' Marla said. She scribbled it down.

Grandma nodded. She looked rather proud about it.

'But who wants you here?' Mum asked.

'That's what we've got to work out,' Grandma said. She looked surprisingly unworried for someone who'd been lured from 5,000 miles away by characters unknown.

'What about the Daughters of Dracula?' Mum asked. 'They hated overseas competition for bloodsucking. Didn't one of them come to see you in Trinidad?'

'Only to tell me that they've all gone vegan.'

'Really?' Mum said. 'So let's presume persons unknown want to bring you back to Peckham. Why now?'

Marla glanced at their laptops lying useless on the sofa. 'It's coming up to our busiest time. So, what if it's about that? Trying to stop something that's happening in the next few weeks.'

'Something or someone.' Grandma and Marla might have the same smile, but Mum and Grandma both pushed their lips into a line when they were thinking hard. 'Who've we got coming over?' Mum asked.

Marla closed her eyes. For some reason it helped her picture what was in her brain better.

'There was Tad Royale,' she said.

'Yes,' Mum agreed. 'We don't want him to get swallowed by an anaconda.' She looked at Grandma. 'What about the Frog Princess and her family?'

Grandma shook her head. 'Ain't got no beef with the frogs.'

'It can't be Puss in Boots,' Mum said. 'He's already posting pictures online. Dancing shoes on and busting some practice moves.'

'Then you said something about a girl in a jar. I didn't have a chance to look at it.'

'Oh,' Mum said. 'Elpis.'

'On its way?' Marla asked. Surely Grandma was enough.

'No!' Mum banged her pencil on the table. It was a very quiet bang. 'Remember the Greek myth? After Pandora took a sneaky look in the jar, and all that nastiness came out into the world, that's who was left. Elpis. Or, in our words, Hope. She emailed last year. She just wanted to come over here and travel around.'

Grandma nodded. 'When the world feels bleak, we need Hope.'

Marla looked down at her notepad. All she'd written down was 'Grandma' and 'Hope'. She held it up. 'It still doesn't make sense.'

'No,' Grandma said. 'It doesn't. Is there anything else that's happened recently? Anything that doesn't feel right?'

That was hard one. Marla was a soucouyant. Stepping out of her skin and turning into a ball of fire wouldn't 'feel right' to virtually everyone else she knew. Grandma and Mum were talking about the night flights and whether Mum had spotted anything unusual in her journeys.

'What about those magpies, Grandma?' Marla asked. 'Wasn't it weird that they attacked you just now?'

Grandma made a face. 'You'd be surprised, honey. That's why I always say 'hot' or 'not', you're either flying fire or a grounded human. When you're something in between, you never know what attention you'll attract. I had this run in with some myna birds in Madagascar once and they...' She rubbed her ear. 'Major hazards, those mynas. Alvi, you really do need to get that lift sorted, though. It was never like that when I was here.'

'It's recent,' Mum said. 'I keep reporting it. It works for an hour or so, then breaks down again. So it's up and down those stairs for us. When you've got a big load of shopping it feels like you're climbing forever. Up and down. Up and down.'

'It must feel like an eternity,' Grandma smiled.

'It's not funny, Mama!'

'Oh, it is,' Grandma said. 'It's funny because I think I know what this is about. I should have guessed what was going on long ago.'

'You've only been here six hours,' Marla said.

'And I've wasted five and a half of them. Let's go.'

The all-night hour bowling alley was off a narrow street that ran by the back of St Thomas' Hospital by London Bridge. Marla had passed the towering glass Shard on night flights before; it was always so different to see it from ground level. It was like a glowing beacon above the bowling alley – though most folk would have no idea the alley existed. It was a renowned chill out spot for FML folk over this side, especially the ones who hadn't acquired the right visas before visiting. They didn't want to advertise their presence. (Apart from 87-storey illuminated glass finger above it, of course.)

Marla, Mum and Grandma took the steps down towards a low path by Thames. Mum glanced around then quickly lifted a small trapdoor that seemed to belong to the Open Sesame pub next door. They trooped through the gloom down the steps and into the reception. Mum nodded to an elf who was patching up some bowling shoes.

'You all right, Youse?'

Youse the elf nodded.

'He in there?'

Youse rolled his eyes. 'Always.'

All the bowling lanes were occupied but only one by a solitary player. He was a bony man with a knee-length beard wearing a Nike sweatsuit.

A black bowling bag sat on a stall next to him. The man was taking bowling balls from it and feeding them along the alley as if they were coins into a slot-machine. He was barely looking to see if he struck anything before sending the next one along.

Grandma marched up to him. 'Sisyphus!'

Sisyphus grunted. Another ball shot down the polished wood. It skidded off into the gutter. Grandma planted herself in front of him. For a moment, Marla thought he was going to bowl her right over. He obviously thought about it too. But then he saw Grandma's face. She had THAT expression. Meanwhile, Mum was having a good old peek into the bowling bag.

'You know why we're here!' Grandma said.

Sisyphus tried to dodge round Grandma to fling the bowling ball, but Grandma leapt in front of him again. The bowling ball thumped to the floor.

'This is harassment!' He cried. 'I haven't done anything wrong!'

'Haven't you?' Mum plucked a small bottle of murky liquid out of the bowling bag. Marla glimpsed the label: STYX FIX

Mum read the blurb at the back. ''Don't want to shoulder that boulder? Take that break you deserve! Styx Fix will secure your troublesome stone to the top of the hill for a minimum of a week guaranteed.'' Mum waved the bottle. 'I wonder what havoc it can cause on lift machinery?'

Sisyphus grinned. 'As you must know by now, rather a lot actually. You're right. It was me. Do you know what it's like? Pushing that boulder up that hill for eternity? With no hope of it ever reaching the top?' His grin widened. 'So if there's no hope for me, why should there be for you?'

Mum glowered at him. 'I was phoning the council to report the repair every day. Press one to go through to Facilities. Press two to leave a message for the ghost who lives in the basement because there are no real live people to speak to you!' Mum's voice had risen. She looked from Marla to Grandma. They looked back. 'Sorry.'

Sisyphus looked deeply satisfied. 'So, how did you find me?'

'We knew you'd want a rematch,' Grandma said. 'You're never going to miss up a chance to cheat the most famous trickster of them all.'

'Well, firstly,' he scowled. 'I am the most famous trickster of them all. And secondly, I have no idea what you're talking about anyway.'

'Lord Anansi,' Marla said. 'Weren't you playing against him last night?'

'Most certainly not! I always play alone!'

'But the computer hacks! The unhappy ever after stories!'

'Stories? What stories? And 'computer hacks'? I have no idea what that means.'

'But you...'Mum said.

'Sorry!' Sisyphus's grin was so wide he must have needed

Styx Fix to keep his lips attached. 'I fear my vacation has come to an end.'

He hooked his bag over his arm, grabbed the bowling ball from the floor, ran up to the lane and swung his arm back. He bowled – without letting go of the ball. He slid along the lane, his immaculate bowling shoes squeaking against the wood and smashed into the pins at the end. With a bang and a clatter, he was gone.

'STRIKE!' The machine yelled.

Marla, Mum and Grandma climbed back up into the early London evening. It was rush hour and commuters hurried over London Bridge to the train station. The sky was streaked orange and pink. Back in Peckham, the windows in the block opposite would be reflecting back the warmth.

'Well,' Mum said. 'That's the lift mystery solved. I hate to admit it, but I believe that cheating liar when he says he has no idea about the computer hacking. I imagine that the wifi signal isn't that great in hell.'

'So it's home, then?' Marla asked. She wanted to solve the mystery, but oh my, it had been a long time since she's been on a night flight with Grandma. Scorching their way through the dark skies was fun with Mum, but even better with Grandma's ear-burning gossip.

'Not quite yet.' Grandma started walking west along the south bank of the river. 'I think I've worked out the rest of the puzzle.'

They followed Grandma along the cobbled street, then out on to the wider path that took them under Blackfriars Bridge. The tide was so far out that it looked like Marla could almost walk across the riverbed to the other side. Grandma had told her about Mama D'Leau, the guardian of Trinidad's rivers. Did the Thames have her own protector?

'Here,' Grandma said.

They stopped outside the Tate Modern, an enormous old power station that had been turned into an art gallery, and stood looking across at the dome of St Paul's Cathedral as the sky darkened behind it. Footsteps clanked across the metallic Millennium Bridge that joined the cathedral to the Tate.

'That noise reminds me of the pan yard,' Grandma sighed. 'There was one at the bottom of the lane when I was a girl.' She tapped out a beat on the railing. 'Bang! Bang! Bang! All the pan men making oil drums into steel drums for the steelband.' An even bigger sigh. 'It's good to be home, Alvi, but...'

'But sometimes that brain of your needs to remember how sharp it is. Is that so, Madam Suki?'

From nowhere, Lord Anansi was leaning on the railing next to Mum. It may have been the last rays of the setting sun, but his eyes seemed ringed with scarlet. He took Grandma's hand.

'Remember the last time we were here?'

'Of course.' The fond smile Grandma gave Lord Anansi was really similar to the one that Marla thought was saved just for her. 'We were here at the dawn of the new millennium to celebrate your statue!'

'I was your first ever client, Madam Suki. You asked me to model for that French artist. She made that giant metal spider, right here on the banks of the river Thames.'

'And it looked magnificent,' Grandma laughed.

Grandma and Lord Anansi suddenly looked at Marla and Mum, like they'd just remembered that they were there.

'I should have known,' Grandma said, nodding towards Lord Anansi. 'It was Mr Trickster all along.'

'Papa Bois and Mama D'Leau are excellent company,' Lord Anansi said. 'But I know you, Madam Suki! I know that sometimes you miss all this.'

He swept his arms around as if he was trying to bring the whole of London towards them.

'All you needed was a good excuse to come back,' he said.

'And like you didn't need an excuse to cheat old Sisyphus?'

He laughed long and loud. 'I have to keep my brain sharp too, Madam Suki. And weaving the perfect puzzle to bring you back to London was a real test! Are you vexed?'

Grandma raised her eyebrows. 'Not if you take those bad reviews down right now! And make sure all the happy endings are back in the right place.'

'Consider it done, Madam Suki.'

It was fully dark now. Marla felt shivery, like her skin wanted to slip off by itself and set her free. She looked up at the sky. London's sky was never dark.

A hand touched her shoulder. 'It's been a long time since we've flown together,' Grandma said.

Marla felt a stab of excitement. 'Can we go home, now?'

'We don't need to, Marla. Step closer, my darlings.'

Mum and Marla snuggled up to Grandma. Grandma nodded at Lord Anansi. He unbuttoned his long jacket and wrapped it round them. It was warm and tickled and almost felt like it had its own life rippling through it.

'Be quick!' Grandma said.

She started to wriggle free of her skin. Mum and Marla looked at each other and then quickly followed suit. The jacket lining bulged and a pocket opened up. They rolled up their skins carefully and one by one, nestled them in the pocket.

'Keep them safe!' Grandma called. 'I don't want no muddle up!'

'Trust me, Madam Suki!'

'Hmmm.'

Marla felt the energy bursting through her. Double, no triple, with her mother and grandmother by her side.

'Are you ready?' Grandma said.

Marla and Mum nodded.

Lord Anansi opened his jacket. For a moment, Marla felt the sharp breeze from the river before she was soaring and soaring. Three bright sparks of intertwined light, following the Thames east over the rainbow scatter of colours from the boats and bridges, past the orange arches of the Thames Barrier, then out over the lightboats to the stars and the sea.

AUTHORS & ILLUSTRATORS

Alexandra Sheppard is an author from North London. Her debut novel *Oh My Gods* was published by Scholastic.

Dorcas Magbadelo is the owner and illustrator behind DorcasCreates. She is passionate about representing and uplifting Black people, specifically Black women, through illustration that includes a lot of bold colours, pattern-work and references to her Nigerian heritage.

Joseph Coelho is a multi-award winning children's author. He writes stage plays, picture books, non-fiction and middle grade. He wrote and presented *Teach Poetry* - a 10-part BBC online series that aims to make the writing of poetry fun and accessible to all.

Selom Sunu is a Christian illustrator and character designer who enjoys bringing characters to life visually. He has worked on books with Knights Of and Penguin Random House. He also provides character designs for Animation, with Disney TV and CBeebies among his clients.

Theresa Lola is a British Nigerian poet. She won the 2018 Brunel International African Poetry Prize. She was the 2019/2020 Young People's Laureate for London. Her 2019 debut poetry collection is *In Search of Equilibrium.*

Mohamed Fadera is a French artist living in London. The African and Black characters in his art are heavily influenced by his Senegalese background. He is very proud of his Black heritage, and that pride is reflected in the representation of Black rituals, myths and cultures within his work.

Kereen Getten grew up in Jamaica but now lives in Birmingham with her family. She won the Caribbean Readers Award for her debut novel *When Life Gives You Mangoes* and was featured in Oprah magazine.

Lucy Farfort is an illustrator and writer of Caribbean and English heritage. In 2017 Lucy was awarded first prize for illustration in Faber Children's inaugural FAB Prize. Her illustrations were also selected for the 2019 CLPE Reflecting Realities report.

Em Norry's middle grade fiction about a teen spy, *Amber Undercover*, came out in April (OUP). She also has stories in *The Place for Me: Stories of the Windrush Generation* (Scholastic, June) as well as a story in the upcoming crime and mystery collection, *A Very Merry Murder Club* (Farshore, Oct).

Chanté Timothy's work often explores different themes of diversity. She loves experimenting with movement, expression and storytelling through her characters. Her debut *A Black Woman Did That* by Malaika Adero in 2020 helped kickstart her passion for children's book illustration.

Clare Weze grew up in London and Yorkshire and has British and Nigerian heritage. She is the author of *The Lightning Catcher* (Bloomsbury), and children's books are some of her favourite things in the world. Writing them is a dream come true.

Camilla Ru is a Zimbabwean born illustrator, based in the rainy city of Manchester. Her work incorporates her love of vibrant colours and passion for connecting people. She enjoys exploring various forms of creativity, expanding imaginations and welcoming inspirations from life's experiences.

Dean Atta's poems deal with themes of race, gender, and identity. His debut YA novel, *The Black Flamingo*, is a Stonewall Book Award winner and a CILIP Carnegie Medal Nominee. You can find him online at www.deanatta.com

Olivia Twist is an illustrator, Arts Facilitator and Lecturer from East London. The key threads which can be found in her work are place, the mundane and overlooked narratives. As a practitioner, her aims are to provide her audience with 'the shock of the familiar' and to trigger greater intergenerational discussion.

Jasmine Richards is an author, scriptwriter and founder of Storymix studio. Her first middle-grade novel in the UK is called *The Unmorrow Curse* - out in 2022. She's co-creator of the Aziza's Secret Fairy Door series published by Macmillan.

Wumi "Wumzum" Olaosebikan is a Nigerian-British illustrator, muralist and animator who specialises in character & world design. Wumzum's craft has taken him across 4 continents and takes inspiration from a range of sources: the visual language of comics; the interactivity of video games; the dynamism of graffiti; and the fluidity of the London Jazz scene.

Yomi Ṣode is a Nigerian British writer, performer, and facilitator. He is a recipient of the Jerwood Compton Poetry Fellowship 2019 and has read his poems internationally at various festivals, as well as performed his debut solo show (COAT) to sold-out audiences. His debut poetry collection, *Manorism* will be published in spring 2022 by Penguin Press.

Willkay is an artist, graphic designer and art director with a fresh outlook on multiple subject matters. He studied at Central Saint Martins and London College of Communication.

Patrice Lawrence was brought up in a Trinidadian-Italian family in Sussex, so had no other choice than to be a writer. She writes for adults, children, young people and any passing balls of flame that may be looking for a good read.

Onyinye Iwu is a Nigerian children's book illustrator and author. She was born in Italy where she spent her childhood, then moved to the UK

Sharna Jackson is an author and curator. Her debut novel *High-Rise Mystery* released in 2019 has won numerous awards and accolades including Best Book for Younger Readers at the 2020 Waterstones Book Prize. The sequel, *Mic Drop*, was released in 2020. Sharna lives on a ship in Rotterdam, Netherlands.

Wesley Barnes graduated from Plymouth University in 2019 with a degree in Graphic Design, and has worked in several studios since then. He has worked on a range of fun projects including editorial illustrations, promotional pieces, and now a book cover!

ACKNOWLEDGMENTS

The authors would like to dedicate their stories to:

Dean Atta:

To all at St John the Evangelist Wembley, the church of my childhood. To all LGBTQ+ people of faith.

Joseph Coelho:

For me. The younger me. The little boy desperate to see characters that looked like him in books. Empowered characters, going on adventures and seeking out magic.

Kereen Getten:

Thank you Knights Of for the opportunity to be part of this wonderful anthology alongside some stellar talent. To Booktrust and CLPE thank you for getting our stories into the hands of children.

Patrice Lawrence:

Dedicating this to my Trini family who schooled me in the legends from an early age. Who doesn't want to be a flying ball of flame?

Theresa Lola:

I would like to acknowledge my mother for introducing me to the beauty of reading books.

E.L. Norry:

For everyone: we all have tales to tell. Stories are stitched into our souls. Our stories are not only where we've come from, but where we're going. We can be Happy Here.

Jasmine Richards:

To my children Zach and Tamsin. You are my happy.

Alexandra Sheppard:

For Maxwell.

Yomi Ṣode:

To the Black young people/adults that see themselves in this book. To Noah & Malia especially. I hope you enjoy, laugh, reflect and know that you too can achieve all of this, and more. Big up x

Clare Weze:

Thanks to Eishar and Aimée at Knights Of, everyone at BookTrust, Abi Fellows at The Good Literary Agency, Salma Begum (at Picador) and everyone on the Northern Writers' Awards team.

KNIGHTS OF is all about YOU. We make books for every kind of reader, from every kind of background and hope you'll read more of the great stories we publish. If it's fearless knights riding bikes or solving mysteries with your sister, if great stories are what you're after – we've got them!

The Centre for Literacy in Primary Education is a charity dedicated to working with primary schools to put quality children's literature at the heart of all learning. It is a charity with a worldwide reputation for excellent literacy training, teaching resources and research that supports teachers to raise the literacy achievement of children. In 2018 CLPE published Reflecting Realities, the first ever survey of Ethnic Representation in Children's Literature. This research set out to quantify the extent and quality of the representation of characters of colour in children's books and highlighted the importance of children seeing themselves and their world reflected in the books they read. The research has led to wide ranging debate and sparked and supported real and concerted action and is now published annually. CLPE continues to work with teachers to support them to ensure that every child can find themselves in their school book corners or libraries.

Visit www.clpe.org.uk for further information.

BookTrust is the UK's largest children's reading charity. We are dedicated to getting children reading because we know that children who read are happier, healthier, more empathetic and more creative. They also do better at school. Each year we reach 3.9 million children and families across the UK with books, resources and support to help develop a love of reading.

We believe children should have access to high quality, diverse and inclusive books to read. Our programme BookTrust Represents was established to promote children's authors and illustrators of colour and to shine a spotlight on diverse creators and books within schools.

For more information about BookTrust, to find out how you can arrange an author visit for your school through BookTrust Represents or for book recommendations, resources and ideas to encourage children to keep reading visit www.booktrust.org.uk